The Rich Mrs. Burgoyne

Kathleen Norris

Contents

THE RICH MRS. BURGOYNE

BY

Kathleen Norris

THE RICH MRS. BURGOYNE

KATHLEEN NORRIS

TO KATHLEEN MARY THOMPSON

> Lover of books, who never fails to find
> Some good in every book, your namesake sends
> This book to you, knowing you always kind
> To small things, timid and in need of friends.

> O friend! I know not which way I must look
> For comfort, being, as I am, opprest,
> To think that now our life is only drest
> For show; mean handy-work of craftsman, cook,

Or groom!--We must run glittering like a brook
In the open sunshine, or we are unblest;
The wealthiest man among us is the best:
No grandeur now in nature or in book
Delights us. Rapine, avarice, expense,
This is idolatry; and these we adore:
Plain living and high thinking are no more:
The homely beauty of the good old cause
Is gone; our peace, our fearful innocence.
And pure religion breathing household laws.
--WILLIAM WORDSWORTH.

CHAPTER I

"Annie, what are you doing? Polishing the ramekins? Oh, that's right.
Did the extra ramekins come from Mrs. Brown? Didn't! Then as soon as
the children come back I'll send for them; I wish you'd remind me. Did
Mrs. Binney come? and Lizzie? Oh, that's good. Where are they? Down in
the cellar! Oh, did the extra ice come? Will you find out, Annie? Those
can wait. If it didn't, the mousse is ruined, that's all! No, wait,
Annie, I'll go out and see Celia myself."

Little Mrs. George Carew, flushed and excited, crossed the pantry as
she spoke, and pushed open the swinging door that connected it with the
kitchen. She was a pretty woman, even now when her hair, already
dressed, was hidden under snugly pinned veils and her trim little
figure lost under a flying kimono. Mrs. Carew was expecting the
twenty-eight members of the Santa Paloma Bridge Club on this particular

evening, and now, at three o'clock on a beautiful April afternoon, she was almost frantic with fatigue and nervousness. The house had been cleaned thoroughly the day before, rugs shaken, mirrors polished, floors oiled; the grand piano had been closed, and pushed against the wall; the reading-table had been cleared, and wheeled out under the turn of the stairway; the pretty drawing-room and square big entrance hall had been emptied to make room for the seven little card-tables that were already set up, and for the twenty-eight straight-back chairs that Mrs. Carew had collected from the dining-room, the bedrooms, the halls, and even the nursery, for the occasion. All this had been done the day before, and Mrs. Carew, awakening early in the morning to uneasy anticipations of a full day, had yet felt that the main work of preparation was out of the way.

But now, in mid-afternoon, nothing seemed done. There were flowers still to arrange; there was the mild punch that Santa Paloma affected at card parties to be finished; there was candy to be put about on the tables, in little silver dishes; and new packs of cards, and pencils and score-cards to be scattered about. And in the kitchen--But Mrs. Carew's heart failed at the thought. True, her own two maids were being helped out to-day by Mrs. Binney from the village, a tower of strength in an emergency, and by Lizzie Binney, a worthy daughter of her mother; but there had been so many stupid delays. And plates, and glasses, and punch-cups, and silver, and napkins for twenty-eight meant such a lot of counting and sorting and polishing! And somehow George and the children must have dinner, and the Binneys and Celia and Annie must eat, too.

"Well," thought Mrs. Carew, with a desperate glance at the kitchen clock, "it will all be over pretty soon, thank goodness!"

A pleasant stir of preparation pervaded the kitchen. Mrs. Binney, enormous, good-natured, capable, was opening crabs at one end of the table, her sleeves rolled up, and her gingham dress, in the last stage of age and thinness, protected by a new stiff white apron; Celia, Mrs. Carew's cook, was sitting opposite her, dismembering two cold roasted fowls; Lizzie Binney, as trim and pretty as her mother was shapeless and plain, was filling silver bonbon-dishes with salted nuts.

"How is everything going, Celia?" said Mrs. Carew, sampling a nut.

"Fine," said Celia placidly. "He didn't bring but two bunches of sullery, so I don't know will I have enough for the salad. They sent the cherries. And Mrs. Binney wants you should taste the punch."

"It's sweet now," said Mrs. Binney, as Mrs. Carew picked up the big mixing-spoon, "but there's the ice to go in."

"Delicious! not one bit too sweet," Mrs. Carew pronounced. "You know that's to be passed around in the little glasses, Lizzie, while we're playing; and a cherry and a piece of pineapple in every glass. Did Annie find the doilies for the big trays? Yes. I got the bowl down; Annie's going to wash it. Oh, the cakes came, didn't they? That's good. And the cream for coffee; that ought to go right on ice. I'll telephone for more celery."

"There's some of these napkins so mussed, laying in the drawer," said Lizzie, "I thought I'd put a couple of irons on and press them out."

"If you have time, I wish you would," Mrs. Carew said, touching the frosted top of an angel-cake with a tentative finger. "I may have to play to-night, Celia," she went on, to her own cook, "but you girls can manage everything, can't you? Dinner really doesn't matter--scrambled eggs and baked potatoes, something like that, and you'll have to serve it on the side porch."

"Oh, yes'm, we'll manage!" Celia assured her confidently. "We'll clear up here pretty soon, and then there's nothing but the sandwiches to do."

Mrs. Carew went on her way comforted. Celia was not a fancy cook, she reflected, passing through the darkened dining-room, where the long table had been already set with a shining cloth, and where silver and glass gleamed in the darkness, but Celia was reliable. And for a woman with three children, a large house, and but one other maid, Celia was a treasure.

She telephoned the grocer, her eyes roving critically over the hall as she did so. The buttercups, in a great bowl on the table, were already dropping their varnished yellow leaves; Annie must brush those up the very last thing.

"So far, so good!" said Mrs. Carew, straightening the rug at the door with a small heel and dropping wearily into a porch rocker. "There must be one thousand things I ought to be doing," she said, resting her head and shutting her eyes.

It was a warm, delicious afternoon. The little California town lay asleep under a haze of golden sunshine. The Carews' pretty house, with its lawn and garden, was almost the last on River Street, and stood on the slope of a hill that commanded all Santa Paloma Valley. Below it, the wide tree-shaded street descended between other unfenced lawns and other handsome homes.

This was the aristocratic part of the town. The Willard Whites' immense colonial mansion was here; and the Whites, rich, handsome, childless, clever, and nearing the forties, were quite the most prominent people of Santa Paloma. The Wayne Adamses, charming, extravagant young people, lived near; and the Parker Lloyds, who were suspected of hiding rather serious money troubles under their reckless hospitality and unfailing

gaiety, were just across the street. On River Street, too, lived
dignified, aristocratic old Mrs. Apostleman and nervous, timid Anne
Pratt and her brother Walter, whose gloomy, stately old mansion was one
of the finest in town. Up at the end of the street were the Carews, and
the shabby comfortable home of Dr. and Mrs. Brown, and the neglected
white cottage where Barry Valentine and his little son Billy and a
studious young Japanese servant led a rather shiftless existence. And
although there were other pretty streets in town, and other pleasant
well-to-do women who were members of church and club, River Street was
unquestionably THE street, and its residents unquestionably THE people
of Santa Paloma.

Beyond these homes lay the business part of the town, the railway
station, and post-office, the library, and the women's clubhouse, with
its red geraniums, red-tiled roof, and plaster arches.

And beyond again were blocks of business buildings, handsome and
modern, with metal-sheathed elevators, and tiled vestibules, and heavy,
plate-glass windows on the street. There was a drug store quite modern
enough to be facing upon Forty-second Street and Broadway, instead of
the tree-shaded peace of Santa Paloma's main street. At its cool and
glittering fountain indeed, a hundred drinks could be mixed of which
Broadway never even heard. And on Broadway, three thousand miles away,
the women who shopped were buying the same boxed powders, the same
bottled toilet waters, the same patented soaps and brushes and candies
that were to be found here. And in the immense grocery store nearby
there were beautifully spacious departments worthy of any great city,
devoted to rare fruits, and coffees and teas, and every pickle that
ever came in a glass bottle, and every little spiced fish that ever
came in a gay tin. A white-clad young man "demonstrated" a cake-mixer,
a blue-clad young woman "demonstrated" jelly-powders.

Nearby were the one or two big dry-goods stores, with lovely gowns in their windows, and milliners' shops, with French hats in their smart Paris boxes--there was even a very tiny, very elegant little shop where pastes and powders and shampooing were the attraction; a shop that had a French name "et Cie" over the door.

In short, there were modern women, and rich women, in Santa Paloma, as these things unmistakably indicated. Where sixty years ago there had been but a lonely outpost on a Spanish sheep-ranch, and where thirty years after that there was only a "general store" at a crossroads, now every luxury in the world might be had for the asking.

All this part of the town lay northeast of the sleepy little Lobos River, which cut Santa Paloma in two. It was a pretty river, a boiling yellow torrent in winter, but low enough in the summer-time for the children to wade across the shallows, and shaded all along its course by overhanging maples, and willows, and oaktrees, and an undergrowth of wild currant and hazel bushes and blackberry vines. Across the river was Old Paloma, where dust from the cannery chimneys and soot from the railway sheds powdered an ugly shabby settlement of shanties and cheap lodging-houses. Old Paloma was peppered thick with saloons, and flavored by them, and by the odor of frying grease, and by an ashy waste known as the "dump." Over all other odors lay the sweet, cloying smell of crushed grapes from the winery and the pungent odor from the tannery of White & Company. The men, and boys, and girls of the settlement all worked in one or another of these places, and the women gossiped in their untidy doorways. Above the Carew house and Doctor Brown's, opposite, River Street came perforce to an end, for it was crossed at this point by an old-fashioned wooden fence of slender, rounded pickets. In the middle of the fence was a wide carriage gate, with a smaller gate for foot passengers at each side, and beyond it the shabby, neglected garden and the tangle of pepper, and eucalyptus, and weeping willow trees that half hid the old Holly mansion. Once this had been the great house of the village, but now it was empty and forlorn.

Captain Holly had been dead for five or six years, and the last of the sons and daughters had gone away into the world. The house, furnished just as they had left it, was for sale, but the years went by, and no buyer appeared; and meantime the garden flowers ran wild, the lawns were dry and brown, and the fence was smothered in coarse rose vines and rampant wild blackberry vines. Dry grass and yarrow and hollow milkweed grew high in the gateways, and when the village children went through them to prowl, as children love to prowl, about the neglected house and orchard, they left long, dusty wakes in the crushed weeds. Further up than the children usually ventured, there was an old bridge across the Lobos, Captain Holly's private road to the mill town; but it was boarded across now, and hundreds of chipmunks nested in it, and whisked about it undisturbed. The great stables and barns stood empty; the fountains were long gone dry. Only the orchard continued to bear heavily.

The Holly estate ran up into the hill behind it, one of the wooded foothills that encircled all Santa Paloma, as they encircle so many California towns. Already turning brown, and crowned with dense, low groves of oak, and bay, and madrona trees, they shut off the world outside; although sometimes on a still day the solemn booming of the ocean could be heard beyond them, and a hundred times a year the Pacific fogs came creeping over them long before dawn, and Santa Paloma awakened in an enveloping cloud of soft mist. Here and there the slopes of these hills were checkered with the sharp oblongs and angles of young vineyards, and hidden by the thickening green of peach and apple orchards. A few low, brown dairy ranch-houses were perched high on the ridges; the red-brown moving stream of the cattle home-coming in mid-afternoon could be seen from the village on a clear day. And over hill and valley, on this wonderful afternoon in late spring, the most generous sunlight in the world lay warm and golden, and across them the shadows of high clouds--for there had been rain in the night--traveled slowly.

"I declare," said little Mrs. Carew lazily, "I could go to sleep!"

CHAPTER II

A moment later when a tall man came up the path and dropped on the top porch step with an air of being entirely at home, Mrs. Carew was still dreaming, half-awake and half-asleep.

"Hello, Jeanette!" said the newcomer. "What's new with thee, coz?"

"Don't smoke there, Barry, and get things mussy!" said Mrs. Carew in return, smiling to soften the command, and to show Barry Valentine that he was welcome.

Barry was usually welcome everywhere, although not at all approved in many cases, and criticised even by the people who liked him best. He was a sort of fourth cousin of Mrs. Carew, who sometimes felt herself called to the difficult task of defending him because of the distant kinship. He was very handsome, lean, and dark, with a sleepy smile and with eyes that all children loved; and he was clever, or, at least, everyone believed him to be so; and he had charm--a charm of sheer sweetness, for he never seemed to be particularly anxious to please. Barry was very gallant, in an impersonal sort of way: he took a keen, elder-brotherly sort of interest in every pretty girl in the village, and liked to discuss their own love affairs with them, with a seriousness quite paternal. He never singled any girl out for particular attention, or escorted one unless asked, but he was flatteringly attentive to all the middle-aged people of his acquaintance and his big helpful hand was always ready for stumbling old women on the church steps, or tearful waifs in the street--he always had time to listen to other people's troubles. Barry--everyone admitted--had his points. But after all--

After all, he was lazy, and shiftless, and unambitious: he was content to be assistant editor of the Mail; content to be bullied and belittled by old Rogers; content to go on his own idle, sunny way, playing with his small, chubby son, foraging the woods with a dozen small boys at his heels, working patiently over a broken gopher-trap or a rusty shotgun, for some small admirer. Worst of all, Barry had been intemperate, years ago, and there were people who believed that his occasional visits to San Francisco, now, were merely excuses for revels with his old newspaper friends there.

And yet, he had been such a brilliant, such a fiery and ambitious boy! All Santa Paloma had taken pride in the fact that Barry Valentine, only twenty, had been offered the editorship of the one newspaper of Plumas, a little town some twelve miles away, and had prophesied a triumphant progress for him, to the newspapers of San Francisco, of Chicago, of New York! But Barry had not been long in Plumas when he suddenly married Miss Hetty Scott of that town, and in the twelve years that had passed since then the golden dreams for his future had vanished one by one, until to-day found him with no one to believe in him--not even himself.

Hetty Scott was but seventeen when Barry met her, and already the winner in two village contests for beauty and popularity. After their marriage she and Barry went to San Francisco, and shrewd, little, beautiful Hetty found herself more admired than ever, and began to talk of the stage. After that, Santa Paloma heard only occasional rumors: Barry had a position on a New York paper, and Hetty was studying in a dramatic school; there was a baby; there were financial troubles, and Barry was drinking again; then Hetty was dead, and Barry, fearing the severe eastern winters for the delicate baby, was coming back to Santa Paloma. So back they came, and there had been no indication since, that the restless, ambitious Barry of years ago was not dead forever.

"No smoking?" said Barry now, good-naturedly. "That's so; you've got some sort of 'High Jinks' on for to-night, haven't you? I brought up those hinges for your mixing table, Jen," he went on, "but any time will do. I suppose the kitchen is right on the fault, as it were."

"The kitchen DOES look earthquakey," admitted Mrs. Carew with a laugh, "but the girls would be glad to have the extra table; so go right ahead. I'll take you out in a second. I have been on the GO," she added wearily, "since seven this morning: my feet are like balls of fire. You don't know what the details are. Why, just tying up the prizes takes a good HOUR!"

"Anything go wrong?" asked the man sympathetically.

"Oh, no; nothing particular. But you know how a house has to LOOK! Even the bathrooms, and our room, and the spare room--the children do get things so mussed. It all sounds so simple; but it takes such a time."

"Well, Annie--doesn't she do these things?"

"Oh, ordinarily she does! But she was sweeping all morning, we moved things about so last night, and there was china, and glasses to get down, and the porches--"

"But, Jeanette," said Barry Valentine patiently, "don't you keep this house clean enough ordinarily without these orgies of cleaning the minute anybody comes in? I never knew such a house for women to open windows, and tie up curtains, and put towels over their hair, and run around with buckets of cold suds. Why this extra fuss?"

"Well, it's not all cleaning," said Mrs. Carew, a little annoyed. "It's largely supper; and I'm not giving anything LIKE the suppers Mrs. White and Mrs. Adams give."

"Why don't they eat at home?" said Mr. Valentine hospitably. "What do they come for anyway? To see the house or each other's clothes, or to eat? Women are funny at a card party," he went on, always ready to expand an argument comfortably. "It takes them an hour to settle down and see how everyone else looks, and whether there happens to be a streak of dust under the piano; and then when the game is just well started, a maid is nudging you in the elbow to take a plate of hot chicken, and another, on the other side, is holding out sandwiches, and all the women are running to look at the prizes. Now when men play cards--"

"Oh, Barry, don't get started!" his cousin impatiently implored. "I'm too tired to listen. Come out and fix the table."

"Wish I could really help you," said Barry, as they crossed the hall; and as a further attempt to soothe her ruffled feelings, he added amiably, "The place looks fine. The buttercups came up, didn't they?"

"Beautifully! You were a dear to get them," said Mrs. Carew, quite mollified.

Welcomed openly by all four maids, Barry was soon contentedly busy with screws and molding-board, in a corner of the sunny kitchen. He and Mrs. Binney immediately entered upon a spirited discussion of equal suffrage, to the intense amusement of the others, who kept him supplied with sandwiches, cake and various other dainties. The little piece of work was presently finished to the entire satisfaction of everyone, and Barry had pocketed his tools, and was ready to go, when Mrs. Carew returned to the kitchen wide-eyed with news.

"Barry," said she, closing the door behind her, "George is here!"

"Well, George has a right here," said Barry, as the lady cast a cautious glance over her shoulder.

"But listen," his cousin said excitedly; "he thinks he has sold the Holly house!"

"Gee whiz!" said Barry simply.

"To a Mrs. Burgoyne," rushed on Mrs. Carew. "She's out there with George on the porch now; a widow, with two children, and she looks so sweet. She knows the Hollys. Oh, Barry, if she only takes it; such a dandy commission for George! He's terribly excited himself. I can tell by the calm, bored way she's talking about it."

"Who is she? Where'd she come from?" demanded Barry.

"From New York. Her father died last year, in Washington, I think she said, and she wants to live quietly somewhere with the children. Barry, will you be an angel?"

"Eventually, I hope to," said Mr. Valentine, grinning, but she did not hear him.

"Could you, WOULD you, take her over the place this afternoon, Barry? She seems sure she wants it, and George feels he must get back to the office to see Tilden. You know he's going to sign for a whole floor of the Pratt Building to-day. George can't keep Tilden waiting, and it won't be a bit hard for you, Barry. George says to promise her anything. She just wants to see about bathrooms, and so on. Will you,

Barry?"

"Sure I will," said the obliging Barry. And when Mrs. Carew asked him if he would like to go upstairs and brush up a little, he accepted the delicate reflection upon the state of his hair and hands, and said "sure" again.

CHAPTER III

Mrs. Burgoyne was a sweet-faced, fresh-looking woman about thirty-two or-three years old, with a quick smile, like a child's, and blue eyes, set far apart, with a little lift at the corners, that, under level heavy brows, gave a suggestion of something almost Oriental to her face. She was dressed simply in black, and a transparent black veil, falling from her wide hat and flung back, framed her face most becomingly in square crisp folds.

She and Barry presently walked up River Street in the mellow afternoon sunlight, and through the old wooden gates of the Holly grounds. On every side were great high-flung sprays of overgrown roses, dusty and choked with weeds, ragged pepper tassels dragged in the grass, and where the path lay under the eucalyptus trees it was slippery with the dry, crescent-shaped leaves. Bees hummed over rank poppies and tangled honeysuckle; once or twice a hummingbird came through the garden on some swift, whizzing journey, and there were other birds in the trees, little shy brown birds, silent but busy in the late afternoon. Close to the house an old garden faucet dripped and dripped, and a noisy, changing group of the brown birds were bathing and flashing about it. The old Hall stood on a rise of ground, clear of the trees, and bathed in sunshine. It was an ugly house, following as it did the fashion of the late seventies; but it was not undignified, with its big door flanked by bay-windows and its narrow porch bounded by a fat wooden balustrade and heavy columns. The porch and steps were weather-stained and faded, and littered now with fallen leaves and twigs.

Barry opened the front door with some difficulty, and they stepped into the musty emptiness of the big main hall. There was a stairway at the back of the house with a colored glass window on the landing, and through it the sunlight streamed, showing the old velvet carpet in the hall below, and the carved heavy walnut chairs and tables, and the old engravings in their frames of oak and walnut mosaic. The visitors peeped into the old library, odorous of unopened books, and with great curtains of green rep shutting out the light, and into the music room behind it, cold even on this warm day, with a muffled grand piano drawn free of the walls, and near it two piano-stools, upholstered in blue-fringed rep, to match the curtains and chairs. They went across the hall to the long, dim drawing room, where there was another velvet carpet, dulled to a red pink by time, and muffled pompous sofas and chairs, and great mirrors, and "sets" of candlesticks and vases on the mantels and what-nots. The windows were shuttered here, the air lifeless. Barry, in George Carew's interest, felt bound to say that "they would clear all this up, you know; a lot of this stuff could be stored."

"Oh, why store it? It's perfectly good," the lady answered absently.

Presently they went out to the more cheerful dining-room, which ran straight across the house, and was low-ceiled, with pleasant square-paned windows on two sides.

"This was the old house," explained Barry; "they added on the front part. You could do a lot with this room."

"Do you still smell spice, and apples, and cider here?" said Mrs. Burgoyne, turning from an investigation of the china-closet, with a radiant face. A moment later she caught her breath suddenly, and walked across the room to stand, resting her hands on a chair back, before a large portrait that hung above the fireplace. She stood so, gazing at the picture--the portrait of a woman--for a full minute, and when she turned again to Barry, her eyes were bright with tears.

"That's Mrs. Holly," said she. "Emily said that picture was here." And turning back to the canvas, she added under her breath, "You darling!"

"Did you know her?" Barry asked, surprised.

"Did I know her!" Mrs. Burgoyne echoed softly, without turning. "Yes, I knew her," she added, almost musingly. And then suddenly she said, "Come, let's look upstairs," and led the way by the twisted sunny back stairway, which had a window on every landing and Crimson Rambler roses pressing against every window. They looked into several bedrooms, all dusty, close, sunshiny. In the largest of these, a big front corner room, carpeted in dark red, with a black marble fireplace and an immense walnut bed, Mrs. Burgoyne, looking through a window that she had opened upon the lovely panorama of river and woods, said suddenly:

"This must be my room, it was hers. She was the best friend, in one way, that I ever had--Mrs. Holly. How happy I was here!"

"Here?" Barry echoed.

At his tone she turned, and looked keenly at him, a little smile playing about her lips. Then her face suddenly brightened.

"Barry, of course!" she exclaimed. "I KNEW I knew you, but the 'Mr. Valentine' confused me." And facing him radiantly, she demanded, "Who am I?"

Barry shook his head slowly, his puzzled, smiling eyes on hers. For a moment they faced each other; then his look cleared as hers had done, and their hands met as he said boyishly:

"Well, I will be hanged! Jappy Frothingham!"

"Jappy Frothingham!" she echoed joyously. "But I haven't heard that name for twenty years. And you're the boy whose father was a doctor, and who helped us build our Indian camp, and who had the frog, and fell off the roof, and killed the rattlesnake."

"And you're the girl from Washington who could speak French, and who put that stuff on my freckles and wouldn't let 'em drown the kittens."

"Oh, yes, yes!" she said, and, their hands still joined, they laughed like happy children together.

Presently, more gravely, she told him a little of herself, of the early marriage, and the diplomat husband whose career was so cruelly cut short by years of hopeless invalidism. Then had come her father's illness, and years of travel with him, and now she and the little girls were alone. And in return Barry sketched his own life, told her a little of Hetty, and his unhappy days in New York, and of the boy, and finally of the Mail. Her absorbed attention followed him from point to point.

"And you say that this Rogers owns the newspaper?" she asked thoughtfully, when the Mail was under discussion.

"Rogers owns it; that's the trouble. Nothing goes into it without the old man's consent." Barry tested the spring of a roller shade, with a scowl. "Barnes, the assistant editor he had before me, threw up his job because he wouldn't stand having his stuff cut all to pieces and changed to suit Rogers' policies," he went on, as Mrs. Burgoyne's eyes demanded more detail. "And that's what I'll do some day. In the six years since the old man bought it, the circulation has fallen off about half; we don't get any 'ads'; we're not paying expenses. It's a crime too, for it's a good paper. Even Rogers is sick of it now; he'd sell for a song. I'd borrow the money and buy it if it weren't for the presses; I'd have to have new presses. Everything here is in pretty good shape," he finished, with an air of changing the subject.

"And what would new presses cost?" Sidney Burgoyne persisted, pausing on the big main stairway, as they were leaving the house a few minutes later.

"Oh, I don't know." Barry opened the front door again, and they stepped out to the porch. "Altogether," he said vaguely, snapping dead twigs from the heavy unpruned growth of the rose vines, "altogether, I wouldn't go into it without ten thousand. Five for the new presses, say, and four to Rogers for the business and good-will, and something to run on--although," Barry interrupted himself with a vehemence that surprised her, "although I'll bet that the old Mail would be paying her own rent and salaries within two months. The Dispatch doesn't amount to much, and the Star is a regular back number!" He stood staring gloomily down at the roofs of the village; Mrs. Burgoyne, a little tired, had seated herself on the top step.

"I wish, in all seriousness, you'd tell me about it," she said. "I am really interested. If I buy this place, it will mean that we come here to stay for years perhaps, and I have some money I want to invest here. I had thought of real estate, but it needn't necessarily be that. It sounds to me as if you really ought to make an effort to buy the paper, Barry, Have you thought of getting anyone to go into it with you?"

The man laughed, perhaps a little embarrassed.

"Never here, really. I went to Walter Pratt about it once," he admitted, "but he said he was all tied up. Some of the fellows down in San Francisco might have come in--but Lord! I don't want to settle here; I hate this place."

"But why do you hate it?" Her honest eyes met his in surprise and reproof. "I can't understand it, perhaps because I've thought of Santa Paloma as a sort of Mecca for so many years myself. My visit here was the sweetest and simplest experience I ever had in my life. You see I had a wretchedly artificial childhood; I used to read of country homes and big families and good times in books, but I was an only child, and even then my life was spoiled by senseless formalities and conventions. I've remembered all these years the simple gowns Mrs. Holly used to wear here, and the way she played with us, and the village women coming in for tea and sewing; it was all so sane and so sweet!"

"Our coming here was the merest chance. My father and I were on our way home from Japan, you know, and he suddenly remembered that the Hollys were near San Francisco, and we came up here for a night. That," said Mrs. Burgoyne in a lower tone, as if half to herself, "that was twenty years ago; I was only twelve, but I've never forgotten it. Fred and Oliver and Emily and I had our supper on the side porch; and afterward they played in the garden, but I was shy--I had never played--and Mrs. Holly kept me beside her on the porch, and talked to me now and then, and finally she asked me if I would like to spend the summer with her. Like to!--I wonder my heart didn't burst with joy! Father said no; but after we children had gone to bed, they discussed it again. How Emily and I PRAYED! And after a while Fred tiptoed down to the landing, and came up jubilant. 'I heard mother say that what clothes Sidney needed could be bought right here,' he said. Emily began to laugh, and I to cry--!" She turned her back on Barry, and he, catching a glimpse of her wet eyes, took up the conversation himself.

"I don't remember her very well," he said; "a boy wouldn't. She died soon after that summer, and the boys went off to school."

"Yes, I know," the lady said thoughtfully. "I had the news in Rome--a hot, bright, glaring day. It was nearly a month after her death, then. And even then, I said to myself that I'd come back here, some day. But it's not been possible until now; and now," her voice was bright and steady again, "here I am. And I don't like to hear an old friend abusing Santa Paloma."

"It's a nice enough place," Barry admitted, "but the people are--well, you wait until you meet the women! Perhaps they're not much worse than women everywhere else, but sometimes it doesn't seem as if the women here had good sense. I don't mean the nice quiet ones who live out on the ranches and are bringing up a houseful of children, but this River Street crowd."

"Why, what's the matter with them?" asked Mrs. Burgoyne with vivacity.

"Oh, I mean this business of playing bridge four afternoons a week, and running to the club, and tearing around in motor-cars all day Sunday, and entertaining the way they think people do it in New York, and getting their dresses in San Francisco instead of up here," Barry explained disgustedly. "Some of them would be nice enough if they weren't trying to go each other one better all the time; when one gets a thing the others have all got to have it, or have something nicer. Take the Browns, now, your neighbors there--"

"In the shingled house, with the babies swinging on the gate as we came by?"

"Yes, that's it. They've got four little boys. Doctor Brown is a king; everybody worships him, and she's a sweet little woman; but of course she's got to strain and struggle like the rest of them. There's a Mrs. Willard White in this town--that big gray-shingled place down there is their garage--and she runs the whole place. She's always letting the others know that hobbles are out, and everything's got to hang from the shoulder--"

"Very good!" laughed Mrs. Burgoyne, "you've got that very nearly right."

"Willard White's a nice fellow," Barry went on, "except that he's a little cracked about his Packard. They give motoring parties, and of course they stop at hotels way up the country for lunch, and the women have got to have veils and special hats and coats, and so on. Wayne Adams told me it stood him in about thirty dollars every time he went out with the Whites. Wayne's got his own car now; his wife kept at him day and night to get it. But he can't run it, so it's in the garage half the time."

"That's the worst of motoring," said the lady with a thoughtful nod, "the people who sell them think they've answered you when they say, 'But you don't run it economically. If you understood it, it wouldn't cost you half so much!' And the alternative is, 'Get a man at seventy-five dollars a month and save repairing and replacing bills.' Nice for business, Barry, but very much overdone for pleasure, I think. I myself hate those days spent with five people you hardly know," she went on, "rushing over beautiful roads that you hardly see, eating too much in strange hotels, and paying too much for it. I sha'n't have a car. But tell me more about the people. Who are the Adamses? Didn't you say Adams?"

"Wayne Adams; nice people, with two nice boys," he supplied; "but she's like the rest. Wayne lies awake nights worrying about bills, and she gives silver photograph-frames for bridge prizes. That white stucco house where they're putting in an Italian garden, is the Parker Lloyds. Mrs. Lloyd's a clever woman, and pretty too; but she doesn't seem to have any sense. They've got a little girl, and she'll tell you that Mabel never wore a stitch that wasn't hand-made in her life. Lloyd had a nervous breakdown a few months ago--we all knew it was nothing but money worry--but yesterday his wife said to me in all good faith that he was too unselfish, he was wearing himself out. She was trying to persuade him to put Mabel in school and go abroad for a good rest."

Mrs. Burgoyne laughed.

"That's like Jeanette Carew showing me her birthday present," Barry went on with a grin. "It seems that George gave her a complete set of bureau ivory--two or three dozen pieces in all, I guess. When I asked her she admitted that she had silver, but she said she wanted ivory, everybody has ivory now. Present!" he repeated with scorn, "why, she just told George what she wanted, and went down and charged it to him! She's worried to death about bills now, but she started right in talking motor-cars; and they'll have one yet. I'd give a good deal," he finished disgustedly, "to know what they get out of it."

"I don't believe they're as bad as all that," said the lady. "There used to be some lovely people here, and there was a whist club too, and it was very nice. They played for a silver fork and spoon every fortnight, and I remember that Mrs. Holly had nearly a dozen of the forks. There was a darling Mrs. Apostleman, and Mrs. Pratt with two shy pretty daughters--"

"Mrs. Apostleman's still here," he told her. "She's a fine old lady. When a woman gets to be sixty, it doesn't seem to matter if she wastes time. Mrs. Pratt is dead, and Lizzie is married and lives in San

Francisco, but Anne's still here. She and her brother live in that
vault of a gray house; you can see the chimneys. Anne's another," his
tone was cynical again, "a shy, nervous woman, always getting new
dresses, and always on club reception committees, with white gloves and
a ribbon in her hair, frightened to death for fear she's not doing the
correct thing. They've just had a frieze of English tapestries put in
the drawing-room and hall,--English TAPESTRIES!"

"Perhaps you don't appreciate tapestries," said Mrs. Burgoyne, with her
twinkling smile. "You know there is a popular theory that such things
keep money in circulation."

"You know there's hardly any form of foolishness or vice of which you
can't say that," he reminded her soberly; and Mrs. Burgoyne, serious in
turn, answered quickly:

"Yes, you're quite right. It's too bad; we American women seem somehow
to have let go of everything real, in the last few generations. But
things are coming around again." She rose from the steps, still facing
the village. "Tell me, who is my nearest neighbor there, in the white
cottage?" she demanded.

"I am," Barry said unexpectedly. "So if you need--yeast is it, that
women always borrow?"

"Yeast," she assented laughing. "I will remember. And now tell me about
trains and things. Listen!" Her voice and look changed suddenly:
softened, brightened. "Is that children?" she asked, eagerly.

And a moment later four children, tired, happy and laden with orchard
spoils, came around the corner of the house. Barry presented them as
the Carews--George and Jeanette, a bashful fourteen and a
self-possessed twelve, and Dick, who was seven--and his own small dusty

son, Billy Valentine, who put a fat confiding hand in the strange lady's as they all went down to the gate together.

"You are my Joanna's age, Jeanette," said Mrs. Burgoyne, easily. "I hope you will be friends."

"Who will I be friends with?" said little Billy, raising blue expectant eyes. "And who will George?"

"Why, I hope you will be friends with me," she answered laughing; "and I will be so relieved if George will come up sometimes and help me with bonfires and about what ought to be done in the stable. You see, I don't know much about those things." At this moment George, hoarsely muttering that he wasn't much good, he guessed, but he had some good tools, fell deeply a victim to her charms.

Mrs. Carew came out of her own gate as they came up, and there was time for a little talk, and promises, and goodbyes. Then Barry took Mrs. Burgoyne to the station, and lifted his hat to the bright face at the window as the train pulled out in the dusk. He went slowly to his office from the train and attacked the litter of papers and clippings on his desk absent-mindedly. Once he said half aloud, his big scissors arrested, his forehead furrowed by an unaccustomed frown, "We were only kids then; and they all thought I was the one who was going to do something big."

CHAPTER IV

Barry appeared at Mrs. Carew's house a little after midnight to find the card-players enjoying a successful supper, and the one topic of conversation the possible sale of Holly Hall. Barry, suspected of having news of it, was warmly welcomed by the tired, bright-eyed women and the men in their somewhat rumpled evening clothes, and supplied with salad and coffee.

"Is she really coming, Barry?" demanded Mrs. Lloyd eagerly. "And how soon? We have been saying what WONDERS could be done for the Hall with a little money."

"The price didn't seem to worry her," said George Carew.

"Oh, she's coming," Barry assured them; "you can consider it settled."

"Good!" said old Mrs. Apostleman in her deep, emphatic voice. "She'll have to make the house over, of course; but the stable ought to make a very decent garage. Mark my words, me dears, ye'll see some very startling changes up there, before the summer's out."

"The house could be made colonial," submitted Mrs. Adams, "or mission, for that matter."

"No, you couldn't make it mission," Mrs. Willard White decided, and several voices murmured, "No, you couldn't do that." "But colonial--it would be charming," the authority went on. "Personally, I'd tear the whole thing down and rebuild," said Mrs. White further; "but with hardwood floors throughout, tapestry papers, or the new grass papers--like Amy's library, Will--white paint on all the woodwork, white and cream outside, some really good furniture, and the garden made over--you wouldn't know the place."

"But that would take months," said Mrs. Carew ruefully.

"And cost like sixty," added Dr. Brown, at which there was a laugh.

"Well, she won't wait any six months, or six weeks either," Barry predicted. "And don't you worry about the expense, Doctor. Do you know who she IS?"

They all looked at him. "Who?" said ten voices together.

"Why, her father was Frothingham--Paul Frothingham, the inventor. Her husband was Colonel John Burgoyne;--you all know the name. He was quite a big man, too--a diplomat. Their wedding was one of those big Washington affairs. A few years later Burgoyne had an accident, and he was an invalid for about six years after that--until his death, in fact. She traveled with him everywhere."

"Sidney Frothingham!" said Mrs. Carew. "I remember Emily Holly used to have letters from her. She was presented at the English court when she was quite young, I remember, and she used to visit at the White House, too. So THAT'S who she is!"

"I remember the child's visit here perfectly," Mrs. Apostleman said, "tall, lanky girl with very charming manners. Her husband was at St. Petersburg for a while; then in London--was it? You ought to know, Clara, me dear--I'm not sure--Even after his accident they went on some sort of diplomatic mission to Madrid, or Stockholm, or somewhere, remember it perfectly."

"Colonel Burgoyne must have had money," said Mrs. White, tentatively.

"Some, I think," Barry answered; "but it was her father who was rich, of course--"

"Certainly!" approved Mrs. Apostleman, fanning herself majestically. "Rich as Croesus; multi-millionaire."

"Heavens alive!" said Mrs. Lloyd unaffectedly.

"Yes," Willard White eyed the tip of a cigar thoughtfully, "yes, I remember he worked his own patents; had his own factories. Paul Frothingham must have left something in the neighborhood of--well, two or three millions--"

"Two or three!" echoed Mrs. Apostleman in regal scorn. "Make it eight!"

"Eight!" said Mrs. Brown faintly.

"Well, that would be about my estimate," Barry agreed.

"He was a big man, Frothingham," Dr. Brown said reflectively. "Well, well, ladies, here's a chance for Santa Paloma to put her best foot forward."

"What WON'T she do to the Hall!" Mrs. Adams remarked; Mrs. Carew sighed.

"It--it rather staggers one to think of trying to entertain a woman worth eight millions, doesn't it?" said she.

CHAPTER V

From the moment of her arrival in Santa Paloma, when she stood on the station platform with a brisk spring wind blowing her veil about her face, and a small and chattering girl on each side of her, Mrs. Burgoyne seemed inclined to meet the friendly overtures of her new neighbors more than half-way. She remembered the baggage-agent's name from her visit two weeks before--"thank Mr. Roberts for his trouble, Ellen"--and met the aged driver of the one available carriage with a ready "Good afternoon, Mr. Rivers!" Within a week she had her pew in church, her box at the post-office, her membership in the library, and a definite rumor was afloat to the effect that she had invested several thousand dollars in the Mail, and that Barry Valentine had bought the paper from old Rogers outright; and had ordered new rotary presses, and was at last to have a free hand as managing editor. The pretty young mistress of Holly Hall, with her two children dancing beside her, and her ready pleased flush and greeting for new friends, became a familiar figure in Santa Paloma's streets. She was even seen once or twice across the river, in the mill colony, having, for some mysterious reason, immediately opened the bridge that led from her own grounds to that unsavory region.

She was not formal, not unapproachable, as it had been feared she might be. On the contrary, she was curiously democratic. And, for a woman straight from the shops of Paris and New York, her clothes seemed to the women of Santa Paloma to be surprising, too. She and her daughters wore plain ginghams for every day, with plain wide hats and trim serge coats for foggy mornings. And on Sundays it was certainly extraordinary to meet the Burgoynes, bound for church, wearing the simplest of dimity or cross-barred muslin wash dresses, with black stockings and shoes, and hats as plain--far plainer!--as those of the smallest children. Except for the amazing emeralds that blazed beside her wedding ring, and the diamonds she sometimes wore, Mrs. Burgoyne might have been a trained nurse in uniform.

"It is a pose," said Mrs. Willard White, at the club, to a few intimate friends. "She's probably imitating some English countess. Englishwomen affect simplicity in the country. But wait until we see her evening frocks."

It was felt that any formal calling upon Mrs. Burgoyne must wait until the supposedly inevitable session with carpenters, painters, paper-hangers, carpet-layers, upholsterers, decorators, furniture dealers, and gardeners was over at the Hall. But although the old house had been painted and the plumbing overhauled before the new owner's arrival, and although all day long and every day two or three Portuguese day-laborers chopped and pruned and shouted in the garden, a week and then two weeks slipped by, and no further evidences of renovation were to be seen.

So presently callers began to go up to the Hall; first Mrs. Apostleman and Mrs. White, as was fitting, and then a score of other women. Mrs. Apostleman had been the social leader in Santa Paloma when Mrs. White was little Clara Peck, a pretty girl in the High School, whose rich widowed mother dressed her exquisitely, and who was studying French, and could play the violin. But Mrs. Apostleman was an old woman now, and had been playing the game a long time, and she was glad to put the sceptre into younger hands. And she could have put it into none more competent than those of Mrs. Willard White.

Mrs. White was a handsome, clever woman, of perhaps six-or seven-and-thirty. She had been married now for seventeen years, and for all that time, and even before her marriage, she had been the most envied, the most admired, and the most copied woman in the village. Her mother, an insipid, spoiled, ambitious little woman, whose fondest hope was realized when her dashing daughter made a financially brilliant match, had lost no time in warning the bride that the agonies of motherhood, and the long ensuing slavery, were avoidable, and Clara had entirely agreed with her mother's ideas, and used to laughingly assure the few old friends who touched upon this delicate topic, that she herself "was baby enough for Will!" Robbed in this way of her natural estate, and robbed by the size of her husband's income from the exhilarating interest of making financial ends meet, Mrs. White, for seventeen years, had led what she honestly considered an enviable and carefree existence. She bought beautiful clothes for herself, and beautiful things for her house, she gave her husband and her mother very handsome gifts. She was a perfect hostess, although it must be admitted that she never extended the hospitalities of her handsome home to anyone who did not amuse her, who was not "worth while". She ruled her servants well, made a fine president for the local Women's Club, ran her own motor-car very skillfully, and played an exceptionally good game of bridge. She was an authority upon table-linens, fancy needlework, fashions in dress, new salads, new methods in serving the table.

Willard White, as perfect a type in his own way as she was in hers, was very proud of her, when he thought of her at all, which was really much less often than their acquaintances supposed. He liked his house to be nicely managed, spent his money freely upon it, wanted his friends handsomely entertained, and his wine-cellar stocked with every conceivable variety of liquid refreshment. If Clara wanted more servants, let her have them, if she wanted corkscrews by the gross, why, buy those, too. Only let a man feel that there was a maid around to bring him a glass when he came in from golfing or motoring, and a corkscrew with the glass!

As a matter of fact, his club and his office, and above all, his motor-cars, absorbed him. His natural paternal instinct had been diverted toward these latter, and, quite without his knowing it, his cars were his nursery. Willard White had owned the first electric car ever seen in Santa Paloma. Later, there had been half-a-dozen machines, and he loved them all, and spoke of them as separate entities. He spoke of the runs they had made, of the strains they had triumphantly sustained, and he and his chauffeur held low-toned conferences over any small breakage, with the same seriousness that he might have used had Willard Junior--supposing there to have been such a little

person--developed croup, and made the presence of a physician
necessary. He liked to glance across his lawn at night to the
commodious garage, visible in the moonlight, and think of his
treasures, locked up, guarded, perfect in every detail, and safe.

He and Mrs. White always spoke of Santa Paloma as a "jay" town, and
compared it, to its unutterable disadvantage, to other and larger
cities, but still, business reasons would always keep them there for
the greater part of the year, and they were both glad to hear that a
fabulously wealthy widow, and a woman prominent in every other respect
as well, had come to live in Santa Paloma. Mrs. White determined to
play her game very carefully with Mrs. Burgoyne; there should be no
indecent hurry, there should be no sudden overtures at friendship.
"But, poor thing! She will certainly find our house an oasis in the
desert!" Mrs. White comfortably decided, putting on the very handsomest
of her afternoon gowns to go and call formally at the Hall.

Mrs. Burgoyne and the little girls were always most cordial to
visitors. They spent these first days deep in gardening, great heaps of
fragrant dying weeds about them, and raw vistas through the pruned
trees already beginning to show the gracious slopes of the land, and
the sleepy Lobos down beneath the willows. The Carew children and the
little Browns were often there, fascinated by the outdoor work, as
children always are, and little Billy Valentine squirmed daily through
his own particular gap in the hedge, and took his share of the fun with
a deep and silent happiness. Billy gave Mrs. Burgoyne many a heartache,
with his shock of bright, unbrushed hair, his neglected grimed little
hands, his boyish little face that was washed daily according to his
own small lights, with surrounding areas of neck and ears wholly
overlooked, and his deep eyes, sad when he was sad, and somehow
infinitely more pathetic when he was happy. Sometimes she stealthily
supplied Billy with new garters, or fastened the buttons on his blue
overalls, or even gave him a spoonful of "meddy" out of a big bottle,

at the mere sight of which Ellen shuddered sympathetically; a dose
which was always followed by two marshmallows, out of a tin box, by way
of consolation. But further than this she dared not go, except in the
matter of mugs of milk, gingerbread, saucer-pies, and motherly kisses
for any bump or bruise.

The village women, coming up to the Hall, in the pleasant summer
afternoons, were puzzled to find the old place almost unchanged. Why
any woman in her senses wanted to live among those early-Victorian
horrors, the women of Santa Paloma could not imagine. But Mrs. Burgoyne
never apologized for the old walnut chairs and tables, and the old
velvet carpets, and the hopelessly old-fashioned white lace curtains
and gilt-framed mirrors. Even Captain Holly's big clock--"an impossibly
hideous thing," Mrs. White called the frantic bronze horses and the
clinging tiger, on their onyx hillside--was serenely ticking, and the
pink china vases were filled with flowers. And there was an air of such
homely comfort, after all, about the big rooms, such a fragrance of
flowers, and flood of sunny fresh air, that the whole effect was not
half as bad as it might be imagined; indeed, when Mammy Curry, the
magnificent old negress who was supreme in the kitchen and respected in
the nursery as well, came in with her stiff white apron and silver
tea-tray, she seemed to fit into the picture, and add a completing
touch to the whole.

Very simply, very unpretentiously, the new mistress of Holly Hall
entered upon her new life. She was a woman of very quiet tastes,
devoted to her little girls, her music, her garden and her books. With
the negress, she had one other servant, a quiet little New England
girl, with terrified, childish eyes, and a passionate devotion to her
mistress and all that concerned her mistress. Fanny had in charge a
splendid, tawny-headed little boy of three, who played happily by
himself, about the kitchen door, and chased chickens and kittens with
shrieks of delight. Mrs. Burgoyne spoke of him as "Fanny's little

brother," and if the two had a history of any sort, it was one at which she never hinted. She met an embarrassing question with a readiness which rather amused Mrs. Brown, on a day when the two younger ladies were having tea with Mrs. Apostleman, and the conversation turned to the subject of maids.

"--but if your little girl Fanny has had her lesson, you'll have no trouble keepin' her," said Mrs. Apostleman.

"Oh, I hope I shall keep Fanny," said Mrs. Burgoyne, "she comes of such nice people, and she's such a sweet, good girl."

"Why, Lord save us!" said the old lady, repentantly, "and I was almost ready to believe the child was hers!"

"If Peter was hers, she couldn't be fonder of him!" Mrs. Burgoyne said mildly, and Mrs. Brown choked on her tea, and had to wipe her eyes.

In the matter of Fanny, and in a dozen other small matters, the independence of the great lady was not slow in showing itself in Mrs. Burgoyne. Santa Paloma might be annoyed at her, and puzzled by her, but it had perforce to accept her as she stood, or ignore her, and she was obviously not a person to ignore. She declined all invitations for daytime festivities; she was "always busy in the daytime," she said. No cards, no luncheons, no tea-parties could lure her away from the Hall, although, if she and the small girls walked in for mail or were down in the village for any other reason, they were very apt to stop somewhere for a chat on their way home. But the children were allowed to go nowhere alone, and not the smartest of children's parties could boast of the presence of Joanna and Ellen Burgoyne.

Santa Paloma children were much given to parties, or rather their parents were; and every separate party was a separate great event. The little girls wore exquisite hand-made garments, silken hose and white shoes. Professional entertainers, in fashionably darkened rooms, kept the little people amused, and professional caterers supplied the supper they ate, or perhaps the affair took the shape of a box-party for a matinee, and a supper at the town's one really pretty tea-room followed. These affairs were duly chronicled in the daily and weekly papers, and perhaps more than one matron would have liked the distinction of having Mrs. Burgoyne's little daughters listed among her own child's guests. Joanna and Ellen were pretty children, in a well-groomed, bright-eyed sort of way, and would have been popular even without the added distinction of their ready French and German and Italian, their charming manners, their naive references to other countries and peoples, and their beautiful and distinguished mother.

But in answer to all invitations, there came only polite, stilted little letters of regret, in the children's round script. "Mother would d'rather we shouldn't go to a sin-gul party until we are young ladies!" Ellen would say cheerfully, if cross-examined on the subject, leaving it to the more tactful Joanna to add, "But Mother thanks you JUST as much." They were always close to their mother when it was possible, and she only banished them from her side when the conversation grew undeniably too old in tone for Joanna and Ellen, and then liked to keep them in sight, have them come in with the tea-tray, or wave to her occasionally from the river bank.

"We've been wondering what you would do with this magnificent drawing-room," said Mrs. White, on her first visit. "The house ought to take a colonial treatment wonderfully--there's a remarkable man in San Francisco who simply made our house over for us last year!"

"It must have been a fearful upheaval," said Mrs. Burgoyne, sympathetically.

"Oh, we went away! Mr. White and I went east, and when we came back it was all done."

"Well, fortunately," said the mistress of Holly Hall cheerfully, as she sugared Mrs. Apostleman's cup of tea, "fortunately all these things of Mrs. Holly's were in splendid condition, except for a little cleaning and polishing. They used to make things so much more solid, don't you think so? Why, there are years of wear left in these carpets, and the chairs and tables are like rocks! Captain Holly apparently got the very best of everything when he furnished this place, and I reap the benefit. It's so nice to feel that one needn't buy a chair or a bed for ten years or more, if one doesn't want to!"

"Dear, sweet people, the Hollys," said Mrs. White, pleasantly, utterly at a loss. Did people of the nicer class speak of furniture as if it were made merely to be useful? "But what a distinct period these things belong to, don't they?" she asked, feeling her way. "So--so solid!"

"Yes, in a way it was an ugly period," said Mrs. Burgoyne, placidly. "But very comfortable, fortunately. Fancy if he had selected Louis Quinze chairs, for example!"

Mrs. White gave her a puzzled look, and smiled.

"Come now, Mrs. Burgoyne," said she, good-naturedly, "Confess that you are going to give us all a surprise some day, and change all this. One sees," said Mrs. White, elegantly, "such lovely effects in New York."

"In those upper Fifth Avenue shops--ah, but don't you see lovely things!" the other woman assented warmly. "Of course, one could be always changing," she went on. "But I like associations with things--and changing takes so much time! Some day we may think all this quite pretty," she finished, with a contented glance at the comfortable ugliness of the drawing-room.

"Oh, do you suppose we shall REALLY!" Mrs. White gave a little incredulous laugh. She was going pretty far, and she knew it, but as a matter of fact, she was entirely unable to believe that there was a woman in the world who could afford to have what was fashionable and expensive in household furnishings or apparel, and who deliberately preferred not to have it. That her own pretty things were no sooner established than they began to lose their charm for her, never occurred to Mrs. White: she was a woman of conventional type, perfectly satisfied to spend her whole life in acquiring things essentially invaluable, and to use a naturally shrewd and quick intelligence in copying fashions of all sorts, small and large, as fast as advanced merchants and magazines presented them to her. She was one of the great army of women who help to send the sale of an immoral book well up into the hundreds of thousands; she liked to spend long afternoons with a box of chocolates and a book unfit for the touch of any woman; a book that she would review for the benefit of her friends later, with a shocked wonder that "they dare print such things!" She liked to tell a man's story, and the other women could not but laugh at her, for she was undeniably good company, and nobody ever questioned the taste of anything she ever said or did. She was a famous gossip, for like all women, she found the private affairs of other people full of fascination, and, having no legitimate occupation, she was always at liberty to discuss them.

Yet Mrs. White was not at all an unusual woman, and, like her associates, she tacitly assumed herself to be the very flower of American womanhood. She quoted her distinguished relatives on all occasions, the White family, in all its ramifications, supplied the correct precedent for all the world; there was no social emergency to which some cousin or aunt of Mrs. White's had not been more than equal. Having no children of her own, she still could silence and shame many a good mother with references to Cousin Ethel Langstroth's "kiddies", or to Aunt Grace Thurston's wonderful governess.

Personally, Mrs. White vaguely felt that there was something innately indecent about children anyway, the smaller they were the less mentionable she found them. The little emergencies, of nose-bleeds and torn garments and spilled porridge, that were constantly arising in the neighborhood of children, made her genuinely sick and faint. And she had so humorous and so assured an air of saying "Disgusting!" or "Disgraceful!" when the family of some other woman began to present itself with reasonable promptness, that other women found themselves laughing and saying "Disgusting!" too.

Mrs. Burgoyne, like Mrs. White, was a born leader. Whether she made any particular effort to influence her neighbors or not, they could not but feel the difference in her attitude toward all the various tangible things that make a woman's life. She was essentially maternal, wanted to mother all the little living and growing things in the world, wanted to be with children, and talk of them and study them. And she was simple and honest in her tastes, and entirely without affectation in her manner, and she was too great a lady to be either laughed at or ignored. So Santa Paloma began to ask itself why she did this or that, and finding her ways all made for economy and comfort and simplicity, almost unconsciously copied them.

CHAPTER VI

When Mrs. Apostleman invited several of her friends to a formal dinner given especially for Mrs. Burgoyne everyone realized that the newcomer was accepted, and the event was one of several in which the women of

Santa Paloma tried with more than ordinary eagerness to outshine each
other. Mrs. Apostleman herself never entered into competition with the
younger matrons, nor did they expect it of her. She gave heavy, rich,
old-fashioned dinners in her own way, in which her servants were
perfectly trained. It was a standing joke among her friends that they
always ate too much at Mrs. Apostleman's house, there were always seven
or eight substantial courses, and she liked to have the plates come
back for more lobster salad or roast turkey. In this, as in all things,
she was a law unto herself.

But for the other women, Mrs. White set the pace, and difficult to keep
they often found it. But they never questioned it. They admired the
richer woman's perfect house-furnishing, and struggled blindly to
accumulate the same number and variety of napkins and fingerbowls,
ramekins and glasses and candlesticks and special forks and special
knives. The first of the month with its bills, became a horror to them,
and they were continually promising their husbands, in all good faith,
that expenses should positively be cut down.

But what use were good resolves; when one might find, the very next
day, that there were no more cherries for the grapefruit, that one had
not a pair of presentable white gloves for the club, or that the
motor-picnic that the children were planning was to cost them five
dollars apiece? To serve grapefruit without cherries, to wear colored
gloves, or no gloves at all to the club, and to substitute some
inexpensive pleasure for the ride was a course that never occurred to
Mrs. Carew, that never occurred to any of her friends. Mrs. Carew might
have a very vague idea of her daughter's spiritual needs, she might be
an entire stranger to the delicately adjusted and exquisitely
susceptible entity that was the real Jeanette, but she would have gone
hungry rather than have Jeanette unable to wear white shoes to Sunday
School, rather than tie Jeanette's braids with ribbons that were not
stiff and new. She was so entirely absorbed in pursuit of the "correct

thing," so anxious to read what was "being read," to own what was "right", that she never stopped to seriously consider her own or her daughter's place in the universe. She was glad, of course when the children "liked their teacher," just as she had been glad years before when they "liked their nurse." The reasons for such likings or dislikings she never investigated; she had taken care of the children herself during the nurse's regular days "off", but she always regarded these occasions as so much lost time. Mrs. Carew kept her children, as she kept her house, well-groomed, and she gave about as much thought to the spiritual needs of the one as the other. She had been brought up to believe that the best things in life are to be had for money, and that earthly happiness or unhappiness falls in exact ratio with the possession or non-possession of money. She met the growing demands of her family as well as she could, and practised all sorts of harassing private economies so that, in the eyes of the world, the family might seem to be spending a great deal more money than was actually the case. Mrs. Carew's was not an analytical mind, but sometimes she found herself genuinely puzzled by the financial state of affairs.

"I don't know where the money GOES to!" she said, in a confidential moment, to Mrs. Lloyd. They had met in the market, where Mrs. Carew was consulting a long list of necessary groceries.

"Oh, don't speak of it!" said Mrs. Lloyd, feelingly. "That's so, your dinner is tomorrow night, isn't it?" she added with interest. "Are you going to have Lizzie?"

"Oh, dear me, yes! For eight, you know. Shan't you have her?" For Mrs. Lloyd's turn to entertain Mrs. Burgoyne followed Mrs. Carew's by only a few days.

"Lizzie and her mother, too," said the other woman. "I don't know what's the matter with maids in these days," she went on, "they simply can't do things, as my mother's maids used to, for example. Now the four of them will be working all day over Thursday's dinner, and, dear me! it's a simple enough dinner."

"Well, you have to serve so much with a dinner, nowadays," Mrs. Carew said, in a mildly martyred tone. "Crackers and everything else with oysters--I'm going to have cucumber sandwiches with the soup--"

"Delicious!" said Mrs. Lloyd.

"'Cucumbers, olives, salted nuts, currant jelly'", Mrs. Carew was reading her list, "'ginger chutney, saltines, bar-le-duc, cream cheese', those are for the salad, you know, 'dinner rolls, sandwich bread, fancy cakes, Maraschino cherries, maple sugar,' that's to go hot on the ice, I'm going to serve it in melons, and 'candy'--just pink and green wafers, I think. All that before it comes to the actual dinner at all, and it's all so fussy!"

"Don't say one word!" said Mrs. Lloyd, sympathetically. "But it sounds dee-licious!" she added consolingly, and little Mrs. Carew went contentedly home to a hot and furious session in her kitchen; hours of baking, boiling and frying, chopping and whipping and frosting, creaming and seasoning, freezing and straining.

"I don't mind the work, if only everything goes right!" Mrs. Carew would say gallantly to herself, and it must be said to her credit that usually everything did "go right" at her house, although even the maids in the kitchen, heroically attacking pyramids of sticky plates, were not so tired as she was, when the dinner was well over.

But there was a certain stimulus in the mere thought of entertaining Mrs. Burgoyne, and there was the exhilarating consciousness that one of these days she would entertain in turn; so the Santa Paloma housewives exerted themselves to the utmost of their endurance, and one delightful dinner party followed another.

But a dispassionate onlooker from another planet might have found it curious to notice, in contrast to this uniformity, that no two women dressed alike on these occasions, and no woman who could help it wore the same gown twice. Mrs. Brown and Mrs. Carew, to be sure, wore their "little old silks" more than once, but each was secretly consoled by the thought that a really "smart" new gown awaited Mrs. White's dinner; which was naturally the climax of all the affairs. Only the wearers and their dress-makers knew what hours had been spent upon these costumes, what discouraged debates attended their making, what muscular agonies their fitting. Only they could have estimated, and they never did estimate--the time lost over pattern books, the nervous strain of placing this bit of spangled net or that square inch of lace, the hurried trips downtown for samples and linings, for fringes and embroideries and braids and ribbons. The gown that she wore to her own dinner, Mrs. White had had fitted in the Maison Dernier Mot, in Paris;--it was an enchanting frock of embroidered white illusion, over pink illusion, over black illusion, under a short heavy tunic of silver spangles and threads. The yoke was of wonderful old lace, and there was a girdle of heavy pink cords, and silver clasps, to match the aigrette that was held by pink and silver cords in Mrs. White's beautifully arranged hair.

Mrs. Burgoyne's gowns, or rather gown, for she wore exactly the same costume to every dinner, could hardly have been more startling than Santa Paloma found it, had it gone to any unbecoming extreme. Yet it was the simplest of black summer silks, soft and full in the skirt, short-sleeved, and with a touch of lace at the square-cut neck. She arranged her hair in a becoming loose knot, and somehow managed to look noticeably lovely and distinguished, in the gay assemblies. To brighten the black gown she wore a rope of pearls, looped twice about her white throat, and hanging far below her waist; pearls, as Mrs. Adams remarked in discouragement later, that "just made you feel what's the use! She could wear a kitchen apron with those pearls if she wanted to, everyone would know she could afford cloth of gold and ermine!"

With this erratic and inexplicable simplicity of dress she combined the finish of manner, the poise, the ready sympathies of a truly cultivated and intelligent woman. She could talk, not only of her own personal experiences, but of the political, and literary, and scientific movements of the day. Certain proposed state legislation happened to be interesting the men of Santa Paloma at this time, and she seemed to understand it, and spoke readily of it.

"But, George," said Mrs. Carew, walking home in the summer night, after the Adams dinner, "you have often said you hated women to talk about things they didn't understand."

"But she does understand, dearie. That's just the point."

"Yes; but you differed with her, George!"

"Well, but that's different, Jen. She knew what she was talking about."

"I suppose she has friends in Washington who keep her informed," said Mrs. Carew, a little discontentedly, after a silence. And there was another pause before she said, "Where do men get their information, George?"

"Papers, dear. And talking, I suppose. They're interested, you know."

"Yes, but--" little Mrs. Carew burst out resentfully, "I never can make head or tail of the papers! They say 'Aldrich Resigns,' or 'Heavy Blow to Interests,' or 'Tammany Scores Triumph,' and _I_ don't know what it's about!"

George Carew's big laugh rang out in the night, and he put his arm
about her, and said, "You're great, Jen!"

Shortly after Mrs. White's dinner a certain distinguished old artist
from New York, and his son, came to stay a night or two at Holly Hall,
on their way home from the Orient, and Mrs. Burgoyne took this occasion
to invite a score of her new friends to two small dinners, planned for
the two nights of the great Karl von Praag's stay in Santa Paloma.

"I don't see how she's going to handle two dinners for ten people each,
with just that colored cook of hers and one waitress," said Mrs.
Willard White, late one evening, when Mr. White was finishing a book
and a cigar in their handsome bedroom, and she was at her
dressing-table.

"Caterers," submitted Mr. White, turning a page.

"I suppose so," his wife agreed. After a thoughtful silence she added,
"Sue Adams says that she supposes that when a woman has as much money
as that she loses all interest in spending it! Personally, I don't see
how she can entertain a great big man like Von Praag in that
old-fashioned house. She never seems to think of it at all, she never
apologizes for it, and she talks as if nobody ever bought new things
until the old were worn out!"

Her eyes went about her own big bedroom as she spoke. Nothing
old-fashioned here! Even eighteen years ago, when the Whites were
married, their home had been furnished in a manner to make the Holly
Hall of to-day look out of date. Mrs. White shuddered now at the mere
memory of what she as a bride had thought so beautiful: the pale green
carpet, the green satin curtains, the white-and-gold chairs and tables

and bed, the easels, the gilded frames! Seven or eight years later she
had changed all this for a heavy brass bedstead, and dark rugs on a
polished floor, and bird's-eye maple chests and chairs, and all
feminine Santa Paloma talked of the Whites' new things. Six or seven
years after that again, two mahogany beds replaced the brass one, and
heavy mahogany bureaus with glass knobs had their day, with plain net
curtains and old-fashioned woven rugs. But all these were in the
guest-rooms now, and in her own bedroom Mrs. White had a complete set
of Circassian walnut, heavily carved, and ornamented with cunningly
inset panels of rattan. On the beds were covers of Oriental cottons,
and the window-curtains showed the same elementary designs in pinks and
blues.

"She dresses very prettily, I thought," observed Mr. White, apropos of
his wife's last remark.

"Dresses!" echoed his wife. "She dresses as your mother might!"

"Very pretty, very pretty!" said the man absently, over his book.

There was a silence. Then:

"That just shows how much men notice," Mrs. White confided to her
ivory-backed brush. "I believe they LIKE women to look like frumps!"

CHAPTER VII

These were busy days in the once quiet and sleepy office of the Santa
Paloma Morning Mail. A wave of energy and vigor swept over the place,
affecting everybody from the fat, spoiled office cat, who found himself

pushed out of chairs, and bounced off of folded coats with small
courtesy, to the new editor-manager and the lady whose timely
investment had brought this pleasant change about. Old Kelly, the
proof-reader, night clerk, Associated Press manager, and assistant
editor, shouted and swore with a vim unknown of late years; Miss
Watson, who "covered" social events, clubs, public dinners, "dramatic,"
and "hotels," cleaned out her desk, and took her fancy-work home, and
"Fergy," a freckled youth who delighted in calling himself a "cub,"
although he did little more than run errands and carry copy to the
press-room, might even be seen batting madly at an unused typewriter
when actual duties failed, so inspiring was the new atmosphere.

Mrs. Burgoyne had a desk and a corner of her own, where her trim figure
might be seen daily for an hour or two, from ten o'clock until the
small girls came in to pick her up on their way home from school for
luncheon. Barry found her brimming with ideas. She instituted the
"Women's Page," the old familiar page of answered questions, and
formulas for ginger-bread, and brief romances, and scraps of poetry,
and she offered through its columns a weekly cash prize for
contributions on household topics. An exquisite doll appeared in the
window of the Mail office, a doll with a flower-wreathed hat, and a
ruffled dress, and a little parasol to match the dress, and loitering
little girls, drawn from all over the village to study this dream of
beauty, learned that they had only to enter a loaf of bread of their
own making in the Mail contest, to stand a chance of carrying the
little lady home. Beside the doll stood a rifle, no toy, but a genuine
twenty-two Marlin, for the boy whose plans for a vegetable garden
seemed the best and most practical, Mrs. Burgoyne herself talked to the
children when they came shyly in to investigate. "She seems to want to
know every child in the county, the darling!" said Miss Watson to Fergy.

The Valentines, father and son, came into the Mail office one warm June
morning, to find the editor of the "Women's Page" busy at her desk,

with the sunlight lying in a bright bar across her uncovered hair, and a vista of waving green boughs showing through the open window behind her.

"What are you two doing here at this hour?" said Sidney, laying down her pen and leaning back in her chair as if glad of a moment's rest. "Why, Billy!" she added in admiring tones, "let me see you! How very, VERY nice you look!"

For the little fellow was dressed in a new sailor suit that was a full size too large for him, his wild mop had been cut far too close, and a large new hat and new shoes were much in evidence.

"D'you think he looks all right?" said Barry with an anxious wistfulness that went straight to her heart. "He looks better, doesn't he? I've been fixing him up."

"And free sailor waists, and stockings, and nighties," supplemented Billy, also anxious for her approval.

"He looks lovely!" said Sidney, enthusiastically, even while she was mentally raising the collar of his waist, and taking an inch or two off the trousers. She lifted the child up to sit on his father's desk, and kissed the top of his little cropped head.

"We may not express ourselves very fluently," said Barry, who was seated in his own revolving chair and busily opening and shutting the drawers of his desk, "but we appreciate the interest beautiful ladies take in our manners and morals, and the new tooth-brushes they buy us--"

"My dear!" protested Mrs. Burgoyne, between laughter and tears, "Ellen used his old one up, cleaning out their paint-boxes!" And she put her warm hand on his shoulder, and said, "Don't be a goose, Barry!" as unselfconsciously as a sister might. "Where are you two boys going, Billy?" she asked, going back to her own desk.

"'Cool," Billy said.

"He's going over to the kindergarten. I've got some work I ought to finish here," Barry supplemented. "I'll take you across the street, Infant, I'll be right back, Sidney."

"But, Barry, why are you working now?" asked the lady a few minutes later when he took his place at his desk.

"Oh, don't you worry," he answered, smiling; "I love it. The thought of old Rogers' face when he opens his paper every morning does me good, I'm writing this appeal for the new reservoir now, and I've got to play up the Flower Festival."

"I'm not interested in the Flower Festival," said Mrs. Burgoyne good-naturedly, "and the minute it's over I'm going to start a crusade for a girls' clubhouse in Old Paloma. Conditions over there for the girls are something hideous. But I suppose we'll have to go on with the Festival for the present. It's a great occasion, I suppose?"

"Oh, tremendous! The Governor's coming, and thousands of visitors always pour into town. We'll have nearly a hundred carriages in the parade, simply covered with flowers, you know. It's lovely! You wait until things get fairly started!"

"That'll be Fourth of July," Sidney said thoughtfully, turning back to her exchanges, "I'll begin my clubhouse crusade on the fifth!" she added firmly.

For a long time there was silence in the office, except for the rustling of paper and the scratch of pens. From the sunny world out-of-doors came a pleasant blending of many noises, passing wagons, the low talk of chickens, the slamming of gates, and now and then the not unmusical note of a fish-horn. Footsteps and laughing voices went by, and died into silence. The clock from Town Hall Square struck eleven slowly.

"This is darned pleasant," said Barry presently, over his work.

"Isn't it?" said the editor of the "Women's Page," and again there was silence.

After a while Barry said "Finished!" with a great breath, and, leaning back in his chair, wheeled about to find the lady quietly watching him.

"Barry, are you working too hard?" said she, quite unembarrassed.

"Am I? Lord, not I wish the days were twice as long. I"--Barry rumpled his thick hair with a gesture that was familiar to Sidney now--"I guess work agrees with me. By George, I hate to eat, and I hate to sleep; I want to be down here all the time, or else rustling up subscriptions and 'ads.',"

"And I thought you were lazy," said Sidney, finding herself, for the first time in their friendship, curiously inclined to keep the conversation personal, this warm June morning. It was a thing extremely difficult to do, with Barry. "You certainly gave me that impression," she said.

"Yes; but that was two months ago," said Barry, off guard. A second later he changed the topic abruptly by asking, "Did your roses come?"

"All of them," answered Sidney pleasantly. And vaguely conscious of mischief in the air, but led on by some inexplicable whim, she pursued, "Do you mean that it makes such a difference to you, Rogers being gone?"

Barry trimmed the four sides of a clipping with four clips of his shears.

"Exactly," said he briefly. He banged a drawer shut, closed a book and laid it aside, and stuck the brush into his glue-pot. "Getting enough of dinner parties?" he asked then, cheerfully.

"Too much," said Sidney, wondering why she felt like a reprimanded child. "And that reminds me: I am giving two dinners for the Von Praags, you know. I can't manage everybody at once; I hate more than ten people at a dinner. And you are asked to the first."

"I don't go much to dinners," Barry said.

"I know you don't; but I want you to come to this one," said Sidney. "You'll love old Mr. von Praag. And Richard, the son, is a dear! I really want you."

"He's an artist, too, isn't he?" said Barry without enthusiasm.

"Who, Richard?" she asked, something in his manner putting her a little at a loss. "Yes; and he's very clever, and so nice! He's like a brother to me."

Barry did not answer, but after a moment he said, scowling a little, and not looking up:

"A fellow like that has pretty smooth sailing. Rich, the son of a big man, traveling all he wants to, studio in New York, clubs--"

"Oh, Richard has his troubles," Sidney said. "His wife is very delicate, and they lost their little girl... Are you angry with me about anything, Barry?" she broke off, puzzled and distressed, for this unresponsive almost sullen manner was unlike anything she had ever seen in him.

But a moment later he turned toward her with his familiar sunny smile.

"Why didn't you say so before?" he said sheepishly.

"Say--?" she echoed bewilderedly. Then, with a sudden rush of enlightenment, "Why, Barry, you're not JEALOUS?"

A second later she would have given much to have the words unsaid. They faced each other in silence, the color mounting steadily in Sidney's face.

"I didn't mean of ME," she stammered uncomfortably; "I meant of everything. I thought--but it was a silly thing to say. It sounded--I didn't think--"

"I don't know why you shouldn't have thought it, since I was fool enough to show it," said Barry after a moment, coming over to her desk and facing her squarely. Sidney stood up, opposite him, her heart beating wildly. "And I don't know why I shouldn't be jealous," he went on steadily, "at the idea that some old friend might come in here and take you away from Santa Paloma. You asked me if it was old Rogers' going that made a difference to me--"

"I know," interrupted Sidney, scarlet-cheeked. "PLEASE"--

"But you know better than that," Barry went on, his voice rising a little. "You know what you have done for me. If ever I try to speak of

it, you say, as you said about the kid just now, 'My dear boy, I like
to do it.' But I'm going to say what I mean now, once and for all. You
loaned me money, and it was through your lending it that I got credit
to borrow more; you gave me a chance to be my own master; you showed
you had faith in me; you reminded me of the ambition I had as a kid,
before Hetty and all that trouble had crushed it out of me; you came
down here to the office and talked and planned, and took it for granted
that I was going to pull myself together and stop idling, and kicking,
and fooling away my time; and all through these six weeks of rough
sailing, you've let me go up there to the Hall and tell you
everything--and then you wonder if I could ever be jealous!" His tone,
which had risen almost to violence, fell suddenly. He went back to his
desk and began to straighten the papers there, not seeing what he did.
"I never can say anything more to you, Sidney, I've said too much now,"
he said a little huskily; "but I'm glad to have you know how I feel."

Sidney stood quite still, her breath coming and going quickly. She was
fundamentally too honest a woman to meet the situation with one of the
hundred insincerities that suggested themselves to her. She knew she
was to blame, and she longed to undo the mischief, and put their
friendship back where it had been only an hour ago. But the right words
did not suggest themselves, and she could only stand silently watching
him. Barry had opened a book, and, holding it in both hands, was
apparently absorbed in its contents.

Neither had spoken or moved, and Sidney was meditating a sudden,
wordless departure, when Ellen Burgoyne burst noisily into the room.
Ellen was a square, splendid child, always conversationally inclined,
and never at a loss for a subject.

"You look as if you wanted to cry, Mother," said she. "Perhaps you
didn't hear the whistle; school's out. We've been waiting ever so long.
Mother, I know you said you hoped Heaven would not send any more dogs

our way for a long while, but Jo and Jeanette and I found one by the school fence. Mother, you will say it has the most pathetic face you ever saw when you see it. Its ear was bloody, and it licked Jo's hand so GENTLY, and it's such a lit-tul dog! Jo has it wrapped up in her coat. Mother, may we have it? Please, PLEASE--"

Barry wheeled about with his hearty laugh, and Mrs. Burgoyne, laughing too, stopped the eager little mouth with a kiss.

"It sounds as if we must certainly have him, Baby!" said she.

CHAPTER VIII

The new mistress of the Hall, in her vigorous young interest in all things, included naturally a keen enjoyment of the village love affairs, she liked to hear the histories of the old families all about, she wanted to know the occupants of every shabby old surrey that drew up at the post-office while the mail was being "sorted." But if the conversation turned to mere idle talk and speculation, she was conspicuously silent. And upon an occasion when Mrs. Adams casually referred to a favorite little piece of scandal, Mrs. Burgoyne gave the conversation a sudden twist that, as Mrs. White, who was present, said later, "made you afraid to call your soul your own."

"Do you tell me that that pretty little Thorne girl is actually meeting this young man, whoever he is, while her mother thinks she is taking a music lesson?" demanded Mrs. Burgoyne, suddenly entering into the conversation. "There's nothing against him, I suppose? She COULD see him at home."

"Oh, no, he's a nice enough little fellow," Mrs. White said, "but she's a silly little thing, and I imagine her people are very severe with her; she never goes to dances or seems to have any fun."

"I wonder if we couldn't go see the mother, and hint that there is beginning to be a little talk about Katherine," mused Mrs. Burgoyne. "Don't you think so, Mrs. Adams?"

"Oh, my goodness!" Mrs. Adams said nervously, "I don't KNOW anything about it! I wouldn't for the world--I never dreamed--one would hate to start trouble--Mr. Adams is very fond of the Thornes--"

"But we ought to save her if we can, we married women who know how mischievous that sort of thing is," Mrs. Burgoyne urged.

"Why, probably they've not met but once or twice!" Mrs. White said, annoyed, but with a comfortable air of closing the subject, and no more was said at the time. But both she and Mrs. Adams were a little uneasy two or three days later, when, returning from a motor trip, they saw Mrs. Burgoyne standing at the Thornes' gate, in laughing conversation with pretty little Katherine and her angular, tall mother.

"And there is nothing in that story at all," said Mrs. Burgoyne later, to Mrs. Carew.

"I suppose you walked up and said, 'If you are Miss Thorne, you are clandestinely meeting Joe Turner down by the old mill every week!'" laughed Mrs. Carew.

"I managed it very nicely," Mrs. Burgoyne said, "I admired their yellow rose one day, as I passed the gate. Mrs. Thorne was standing there, and I asked if it wasn't a Banksia. Then the little girl came out of the house, and she happened to know who I am--"

"Astonishingly bright child!" said Mrs. Carew.

"Well, and then we talked roses, and the father came home--a nice old man. And I asked him if he'd lend me Miss Thorne now and then to play duets--and he agreed. So the child's been up to the Hall once or twice, and she's a nice little thing. She doesn't care tuppence for the Turner boy, but he's musical, and she's quite music-mad, and now and then they 'accidentally' meet. Her father won't let anyone see her at the house. She wants to study abroad, but they can't afford it, I imagine, so I've written to see if I can interest a friend of mine in Berlin--But why do you smile?" she broke off to ask innocently.

"At the thought of your friend in Berlin!" said Mrs. Carew audaciously. For she was not at all awed by Mrs. Burgoyne now.

Indeed, she and Mrs. Brown were growing genuinely fond of their new neighbor, and the occupants of the Hall supplied them with constant amusement and interest. Great lady and great heiress Sidney Burgoyne might be, but she lived a life far simpler than their own, and loved to have them come in for a few minutes' talk even if she were cutting out cookies, with Joanna and Ellen leaning on the table, or feeding the chickens whose individual careers interested her so deeply. She walked with the little girls to school every morning, and met them near the school at one o'clock. In the meantime she made a visit to the Mail office, and perhaps spent an hour or two there, or in the markets; but at least three times a week she wandered over to Old Paloma, and spent the forenoon in the dingy streets across the river. What she did there, perhaps no one but Doctor Brown, who came to have a real affection and respect for her, fully appreciated. Mrs. Burgoyne would tell him, when they met in some hour of life or death, that she was "making friends." It was quite true. She was the type of woman who cannot pass a small child in the street. She must stop, and ask questions, decide disputes and give advice. And through the children she won the big brothers and sisters and fathers and mothers of Old Paloma. Even a deep-rooted prejudice against the women of her class and their method of dealing with the less fortunate could not prevail against her disarming, friendly manner, her simple gown and hat, her eagerness to get the new baby into her arms; all these told in her favor, and she became very popular in the shabby little settlement across the bridge. She would sit at a sewing-machine and show old Mrs. Goodspeed how to turn a certain hem, she would prescribe barley-water and whey for the Barnes baby, she would explain to Mrs. Ryan the French manner of cooking tough meat, it is true; but, on the other hand, she let pale little discouraged Mrs. Weber, of the Bakery, show her how to make a German potato pie, and when Mrs. Ryan's mother, old Mrs. Lynch, knitted her a shawl, with clean, thin old work-worn hands, the tears came into her bright eyes as she accepted the gift. So it was no more than a neighborly give-and-take after all. Mrs. Burgoyne would fall into step beside a factory girl, walking home at sunset. "How was it today, Nellie? Did you speak to the foreman about an opening for your sister?" the rich, interested voice would ask. Or perhaps some factory lad would find her facing him in a lane. "Tell me, Joe, what's all this talk of trouble between you and the Lacy boys at the rink?"

"I'm a widow, too," she reminded poor little Mrs. Peevy, one day, "I understand." "Do let me send you the port wine I used to take after Ellen was born," she begged one little sickly mother, and when she loaned George Manning four hundred dollars to finish his new house, and get his wife and babies up from San Francisco, the transaction was made palatable to George by her encouraging: "Everyone borrows money for building, I assure you. I know my father did repeatedly."

When more subtle means were required, she was still equal to the occasion. It was while Viola Peet was in the hospital for a burned wrist that Mrs. Burgoyne made a final and effective attempt to move

poor little Mrs. Peet out of the bedroom where she had lain
complaining, ever since the accident that had crippled her and killed
her husband five years before. Mrs. Burgoyne put it as a "surprise for
Viola," and Mrs. Peet, whose one surviving spark of interest in life
centred in her three children, finally permitted carpenters to come and
build a porch outside her dining-room, and was actually transferred,
one warm June afternoon, to the wide, delicious hammock-bed that Mrs.
Burgoyne had hung there. Her eyes, dulled with staring at a chocolate
wall-paper, and a closet door, for five years, roved almost angrily
over the stretch of village street visible from the porch; the
perspective of tree-smothered roofs and feathery elm and locust trees.

"'Tisn't a bit more than I'd do for you if I was rich and you poor,"
said Mrs. Peet, rebelliously.

"Oh, I know that!" said Mrs. Burgoyne, busily punching pillows.

"An', as you say, Viola deserves all I c'n do for her," pursued the
invalid. "But remember, every cent of this you git back."

"Every cent, just as soon as Lyman is old enough to take a job," agreed
Mrs. Burgoyne. "There, how's that? That's the way Colonel Burgoyne
liked to be fixed."

"You're to make a note of just what it costs," persisted Mrs. Peet,
"this wrapper, and the pillers, and all."

"Oh, let the wrapper be my present to you, Mrs. Peet!"

"No, MA'AM!" said Mrs. Peet, firmly. And she told the neighbors, later,
in the delightfully exciting afternoon and evening that followed her
installation on the porch, that she wasn't an object of charity, and
she and Mrs. Burgoyne both knew it. Mrs. Burgoyne would not stay to see

Viola's face, when she came home from the hospital to find her mother watching the summer stars prick through the warm darkness, but Viola came up to the Hall that same evening, and tried to thank Mrs. Burgoyne, and laughed and cried at once, and had to be consoled with cookies and milk until the smiles had the upper hand, and she could go home, with occasional reminiscent sobs still shaking her bony little chest.

"What are you trying to do over there?" asked Dr. Brown, coming in with his wife for a rubber of bridge, as Viola departed. "Whereever I go, I come across your trail. Are we nursing a socialist in our bosom?"

"No-o-o, I don't think I'm that," said Sidney laughing, and pushing the porch-chairs into comfortable relation. "Let's sit out here until Mr. Valentine comes. No, I'm not a socialist. But I can't help feeling that there's SOME solution for a wretched problem like that over there," a wave of the hand indicated Old Paloma, "and perhaps, dabbling aimlessly about in all sorts of places, one of us may hit upon it."

"But I thought the modern theory was against dabbling," said Mrs. Brown, a little timidly, for she held a theory that she was not "smart." "I thought everything was being done by institutions, and by laws--by legislation."

"Nothing will ever be done by legislation, to my thinking at least," Mrs. Burgoyne said. "A few years ago we legislated some thousands of new babies into magnificent institutions. Nurses mixed their bottles, doctors inspected them, nurses turned them and washed them and watched them. Do you know what percentage survived?"

"Doesn't work very well," said the doctor, shaking a thoughtful head over his pipe.

"Just one hundred per cent didn't survive!" said Mrs. Burgoyne. "Now they take a foundling or an otherwise unfortunate baby, and give it to a real live mother. She nurses it if she can, she keeps near to it and cuddles it, and loves it. And so it lives. In all the asylums, it's the same way. Groups are getting smaller and smaller, a dozen girls with a matron in a cottage, and hundreds of girls 'farmed out' with good, responsible women, instead of enormous refectories and dormitories and schoolrooms. And the ideal solution will be when every individual woman in the world extends her mothering to include every young thing she comes in contact with; one doll for her own child and another doll for the ashman's little girl, one dimity for her own debutante, and another just as dainty for the seventeen-year-old who brings home the laundry every week."

"Yes, but that's puttering here and there," asserted Mrs. Brown, "wouldn't laws for a working wage do all that, and more, too?"

"In the first place, a working wage doesn't solve it," Mrs. Burgoyne answered vigorously, "because in fully half the mismanaged and dirty homes, the working people HAVE a working wage, have an amount of money that would amaze you! Who buys the willow plumes, and the phonographs, and the enlarged pictures, and the hair combs and the white shoes that are sold by the million every year? The poor people, girls in shops, and women whose babies are always dirty, and always broken out with skin trouble, and whose homes are hot and dirty and miserable and mismanaged."

"Well, make some laws to educate 'em then, if it's education they all need," suggested the doctor, who had been auditing every clause of the last remark with a thoughtful nod.

"No, wages aren't the question," Mrs. Burgoyne reiterated. "Why, I knew a little Swedish woman once, who raised three children on three hundred dollars a year."

"She COULDN'T!" ejaculated Mrs. Brown.

"Oh, but she did! She paid one dollar a week for rent, too. One son is a civil engineer, now, and the daughter is a nurse. The youngest is studying medicine."

"But what did they EAT, do you suppose?"

"Oh, I don't know. Potatoes, I suppose, and oatmeal and baked cabbage, and soup. I know she got a quart of buttermilk every day, for three cents. They were beautiful children. They went to free schools, and lectures, and galleries, and park concerts, and free dispensaries, when they needed them. Laws could do no more for her, she knew her business."

"Well, education WOULD solve it then," concluded Mrs. Brown.

"I don't know." Mrs. Burgoyne answered, reflectively, "Book education won't certainly. But example might, I believe example would."

"You mean for people of a better class to go and live among them?" suggested the doctor.

"No, but I mean for people of a better class to show them that what they are striving for isn't vital, after all. I mean for us to so order our lives that they will begin to value cleanliness, and simplicity, and the comforts they can afford. You know, Mary Brown," said Mrs. Burgoyne, turning suddenly to the doctor's wife, with her gay, characteristic vehemence, "it's all our fault, all the misery and suffering and sin of it, everywhere!"

"Our fault! You and me!" cried Mrs. Brown, aghast.

"No, all the fault of women, I mean!" Mrs. Burgoyne laughed too as Mrs. Brown settled back in her chair with a relieved sigh. "We women," she went on vigorously, "have mismanaged every separate work that was ever put into our hands! We ought to be ashamed to live. We cumber--"

"Here!" said the doctor, smiling in lazy comfort over his pipe, "that's heresy! I refuse to listen to it. My wife is a woman, my mother, unless I am misinformed, was another--"

"Don't mind him!" said Mrs. Brown, "but go on! What have we all done? We manage our houses, and dress our children, and feed our husbands, it seems to me."

"Well, there's the big business of motherhood," began Mrs. Burgoyne, "the holiest and highest thing God ever let a mortal do. We evade it and ignore it to such an extent that the nation--and other nations--grows actually alarmed, and men begin to frame laws to coax us back to the bearing of children. Then, if we have them, we turn the entire responsibility over to other people. A raw little foreigner of some sort answers the first questions our boys and girls ask, until they are old enough to be put under some nice, inexperienced young girl just out of normal school, who has fifty or sixty of them to manage, and of whose ideas upon the big questions of life we know absolutely nothing. We say lightheartedly that 'girls always go through a trying age,' and that we suppose boys 'have to come in contact with things,' and we let it go at that! We 'suppose there has always been vice, and always will be,' but we never stop to think that we ourselves are setting the poor girls of the other world such an example in the clothes we wear, and the pleasures we take, that they will sell even themselves for pretty gowns and theatre suppers. We regret sweat-shops, even while we patronize the stores that support them, and we bemoan child-labor, although I suppose the simplest thing in the world would be to find out where the cotton goes that is worked by babies, and refuse to buy those brands of cotton, and make our merchants tell us where they DO get their supply! We have managed our household problem so badly that we simply can't get help--"

"You CANNOT do your own work, with children," said Mrs. Brown firmly.

"Of course you can't. But why is it that our nice young American girls won't come into our homes? Why do we have to depend upon the most ignorant and untrained of our foreign people? Our girls pour into the factories, although our husbands don't have any trouble in getting their brothers for office positions. There is always a line of boys waiting for a possible job at five dollars a week."

"Because they can sleep at home," submitted the doctor.

"You know that, other things being equal, young people would much rather not sleep at home," said Mrs. Burgoyne, "it's the migrating age. They love the novelty of being away at night."

"Well, when a boy comes into my office," the doctor reasoned slowly, "he knows that he has certain unimportant things to do, but he sees me taking all the real responsibility, he knows that I work harder than he does."

"Exactly," said Mrs. Burgoyne. "Men do their own work, with help. We don't do ours. Not only that, but every improvement that comes to ours comes from men. They invent our conveniences, they design our stoves and arrange our sinks. Not because they know anything about it, but because we're not interested."

"One would think you had done your own work for twenty years!" said Mrs. Brown.

"I never did it," Mrs. Burgoyne answered smiling, "but I sometimes wish I could. I sometimes envy those busy women who have small houses, new babies, money cares--it must be glorious to rise to fresh emergencies every hour of your life. A person like myself is handicapped. I can't demonstrate that I believe what I say. Everyone thinks me merely a little affected about it. If I were such a woman, I'd glory in clipping my life of everything but the things I needed, and living like one of my own children, as simply as a lot of peasants!"

"And no one would ever be any the wiser," said Mrs. Brown.

"I don't know. Quiet little isolated lives have a funny way of getting out into the light. There was that little peasant girl at Domremy, for instance; there was that gentle saint who preached poverty to the birds; there was Eugenie Guerin, and the Cure of Ars, and the few obscure little English weavers--and there was the President who split--"

"I thought we'd come to him!" chuckled the doctor.

"Well," Mrs. Burgoyne smiled, a little confused at having betrayed hero-worship. "Well, and there was one more, the greatest of all, who didn't found any asylums, or lead any crusade--" She paused.

"Surely," said the doctor, quietly. "Surely. I suppose that curing the lame here, and the blind there, and giving the people their fill of wine one day, and of bread and fishes the next, might be called 'dabbling' in these days. But the love that went with those things is warming the world yet!"

"Well, but what can we DO?" demanded Mrs. Brown after a short silence.

"That's for us to find out," said Mrs. Burgoyne, cheerfully.

"A correct diagnosis is half a cure," ended the doctor, hopefully.

CHAPTER IX

Barry was the last guest to reach Holly Hall on the evening of Mrs. Burgoyne's first dinner-party, and came in to find the great painter who was her guest the centre of a laughing and talking group in the long drawing-room. Mrs. Apostleman, with an open book of reproductions from Whistler on her broad, brocade lap, had the armchair next to the guest of honor, and Barry's quick look for his hostess discovered her on a low hassock at the painter's knee, looking very young and fresh, in her white frock, with a LaMarque rose at her belt and another in her dark hair. She greeted him very gravely, almost timidly, and in the new self-consciousness that had suddenly come to them both it was with difficulty that even the commonplace words of greeting were accomplished, and it was with evident relief that she turned from him to ask her guests to come into the dining-room.

Warm daylight was still pouring into the drawing-room at seven o'clock, and in the pleasant dining-room, too, there was no other light. The windows here were wide open, and garden scents drifted in from the recently watered flower-beds. The long table, simply set, was ornamented only by low bowls of the lovely San Rafael roses.

Guided and stimulated by the hostess, the conversation ran in a gay, unbroken stream, for the painter liked to talk, and Santa Paloma enjoyed him. But under it all the women guests were aware of an almost resentful amazement at the simplicity of the dinner. When, after nine o'clock, the ladies went into the drawing-room and settled about a snapping wood fire, Mrs. Lloyd could not resist whispering to Mrs. Apostleman, "For a COMPANY dinner!" Mrs. Adams was entirely absorbed in deciding just what position she would take when Mrs. White alluded to the affair the next day; but Mrs. White had come primed for special business this evening, and she took immediate advantage of the absence of the men to speak to Mrs. Burgoyne.

"As president of our little club," said she, when they were all seated, "I am authorized to ask you if I may put your name up for membership, Mrs. Burgoyne. We are all members here, and in this quiet place our meetings are a real pleasure, and I hope an education as well."

"Oh, really--!" Mrs. Burgoyne began, but the other went on serenely:

"I brought one of our yearly programs, we have just got them out, and I'm going to leave it with you. I think Mr. White left it here on the table. Yes; here it is. You see," she opened a dainty little book and flattened it with a white, jeweled hand, "our work is all laid out, up to the president's breakfast in March. I go out then, and a week later we inaugurate the new president. Let me just run over this for you, for I KNOW it will interest you. Now here, Tuesdays. Tuesday is our regular meeting day. We have a program, music, and books suggested for the week, reports, business, and one good paper--the topics vary; here's 'Old Thanksgiving Customs,' in November, then a debate, 'What is Friendship,' then 'Christmas Spirit,' and then our regular Christmas Tree and Jinks. Once a month, on Tuesday, we have some really fine speaker from the city, and we often have fine singers, and so on. Then we have a monthly reception for our visitors, and a supper; usually we just have tea and bread-and-butter after the meetings. Then, first Monday, Directors' Meeting; that doesn't matter. Every other Wednesday the Literary Section meets, they are doing wonderful work; Miss Foster has that; she makes it very interesting. 'What English Literature Owes to Meredith,' 'Rossetti, the Man,'--you see I'm just skimming, to give you some idea. Then the Dramatic Section, every other Thursday; they give a play once a year; that's great fun! 'Ibsen--Did he Understand

Women?' 'Please Explain--Mr. Shaw?'--Mrs. Moore makes that very amusing. Then alternate Thursdays the Civic and Political Section--"

"Ah! What does that do?" said Mrs. Burgoyne.

"Why," said Mrs. White hesitating, "I haven't been--however, I think they took up the sanitation of the schools; Miss Jewett, from Sacramento, read a splendid paper about it. There's a committee to look into that, and then last year that section planted a hundred trees. And then there's parliamentary drill."

"Which we all need," said Mrs. Adams, and there was laughter.

"Then there's the Art Department once a month," resumed Mrs. White, "Founders' Day, Old-Timers' Day, and, in February, we think Judge Lindsey may address us--"

"Oh, are you doing any juvenile-court work?" said the hostess.

"We wanted his suggestions about it," Mrs. White said. "We feel that if we COULD get some of the ladies interested--! Then here's the French class once a week; German, Spanish, and the bridge club on Fridays."

"Gracious! You use your clubhouse," said Mrs. Burgoyne.

"Nearly every day. So come on Tuesday," said the president winningly, "and be our guest. A Miss Carroll is to sing, and Professor Noyesmith, of Berkeley, will read a paper on: 'The City Beautiful.' Keep that year-book; I butchered it, running through it so fast."

"Well, just now," Mrs. Burgoyne began a little hesitatingly, "I'm rather busy. I am at the Mail office while the girls are in school, you know, and we have laid out an enormous lot of gardening for afternoons.

They never tire of gardening if I'm with them, but, of course, no children will do that sort of thing alone; and it's doing them both so much good that I don't want to stop it. Then they study German and Italian with me, and on Saturday have a cooking lesson. You see, my time is pretty full."

"But a good governess would take every bit of that off your hands, me dear," said Mrs. Apostleman.

"Oh, but I love to do it!" protested Mrs. Burgoyne with her wide-eyed, childish look. "You can't really buy for them what you can do yourself, do you think so? And now the other children are beginning to come in, and it's such fun! But that isn't all. I have editorial work to do, besides the Mail, you know. I manage the 'Answers to Mothers' column in a little eastern magazine. I daresay you've never seen it; it is quite unpretentious, but it has a large circulation. And these mothers write me, some of them factory-workers, or mothers of child-workers even, or lonely women on some isolated ranch; you've no idea how interesting it is! Of course they don't know who I am, but we become good friends, just the same. I have the best reference books about babies and sickness, and I give them the best advice I can. Sometimes it's a boy's text-book that is wanted, or a second-hand crib, or some dear old mother to get into a home, and they are so self-respecting about it, and so afraid they aren't paying fair--I love that work! But, of course, it takes time. Then I've been hunting up a music-teacher for the girls. I can't teach them that--"

"I meant to speak to you of that," Mrs. White said. "There's a Monsieur Posti, Emil Posti, he studied with Leschetizky, you know, who comes up from San Francisco every other week, and we all take from him. In between times--"

"Oh, but I've engaged a nice little Miss Davids from Old Paloma," said

Mrs. Burgoyne.

"From Old Paloma!" echoed three women together. And Mrs. Apostleman added heavily, "Never heard of her!"

"I got a good little Swedish sewing-woman over there," the hostess explained, "and she told me of this girl. She's a sweet girl; no mother, and a little sister to bring up. She was quite pleased."

"But, good heavens! What does she know? What's her method?" demanded Mrs. White in puzzled disapproval.

"She has a pretty touch," Mrs. Burgoyne said mildly, "and she's bristling with ambition and ideas. She's not a genius, perhaps; but, then, neither is either of the girls. I just want them to play for their own pleasure, read accompaniments; something of that sort. Don't you know how popular the girl who can play college songs always is at a house-party?"

"Well, really--" Mrs. White began, almost annoyed; but she broke her sentence off abruptly, and Mrs. Apostleman filled the pause.

"Whatever made ye go over there for a dress-maker?" she demanded. "We never think of going there. There's a very good woman here, in the Bank Building--"

"Madame Sorrel," supplemented Mrs. Adams.

"She's fearfully independent," Mrs. Lloyd contributed; "but she's good. She made your pink, didn't she, Sue? Wayne said she did."

Mrs. Adams turned pink herself; the others laughed suddenly.

"Oh, you naughty girl!" Mrs. White said. "Did you tell Wayne you got that frock in Santa Paloma?"

"What Wayne doesn't know won't hurt him," said his wife. "Sh! Here they come!" And the conversation terminated abruptly, with much laughter.

Mrs. Burgoyne's dinner-party dispersed shortly after ten o'clock, so much earlier than was the custom in Santa Paloma that none of the ordered motor-cars were in waiting. The guests walked home together, absorbed in an animated conversation; for the gentlemen, who were delighted to be getting home early, delighted with a dinner that, as Wayne Adams remarked, "really stood for something to eat, not just things passed to you, or put down in dabs before you," and delighted with the pleasant informality of sitting down in daylight, were enthusiastic in their praise of Mrs. Burgoyne. The ladies differed with them.

"She knows how to do things," said Parker Lloyd. "Old Von Praag himself said that she was a famous dinner-giver."

"I don't know what you'd say, Wayne," said Mrs. Adams patiently, "if _I_ asked people to sit down to the dinner we had to-night! Of course we haven't eight millions, but I would be ashamed to serve a cocktail, a soup--I frankly admit it was delicious--steaks, plain lettuce salad, and fruit. I don't count coffee and cheese. No wines, no entrees; I think it was decidedly QUEER."

"I wish some of you others would try it," said Willard White unexpectedly. "I never get dinners like that, except at the club, down in town. The cocktail was a rare sherry, the steaks were broiled to a turn, and the salad dressing was a wonder. She had her cheese just ripe enough, and samovar coffee to wind up with--what more do you want? I serve wine myself, but champagne keeps you thirsty all night, and other wines put me to sleep. I don't miss wine! I call it a bang-up dinner, don't you, Parker?"

Parker Lloyd, with his wife on his arm, felt discretion his part.

"Well," he said innocently selecting the one argument most distasteful to the ladies, "it was a man's dinner, Will. It was just what a man likes, served the way he likes it. But if the girls like flummery and fuss, I don't see why they shouldn't have it."

"Really!" said Mrs. White with a laugh that showed a trace of something not hilarious, "really, you are all too absurd! We are a long way from the authorities here, but I think we will find out pretty soon that simple dinners have become the fad in Washington, or Paris, and that your marvelous Mrs. Burgoyne is simply following the fashion like all the rest of us."

CHAPTER X

Barry had murmured something about "rush of work at the office" when he came in a few minutes late for Mrs. Burgoyne's dinner, but as the evening wore on, he seemed in no hurry to depart. Sidney was delighted to see him really in his element with the Von Praags, father and son, the awakened expression that was so becoming to him on his face, and his curiously complex arguments stirring the old man over and over again to laughter. She had been vexed at herself for feeling a little shyness when he first came in; the unfamiliar evening dress and the gravity of his handsome face had made him seem almost a stranger, but this wore off, and after the other guests had gone these four still sat laughing and talking like the best of old friends together.

When the Von Praags had gone upstairs, she walked with him to the porch, and they stood at the top of the steps for a moment, the rich scent of the climbing LaMarque and Banksia roses heavy about them, and the dark starry arch of the sky above. Sidney, a little tired, but pleased with her dinner and her guests, and ready for a breath of the sweet summer night before going upstairs, was confused by having her heart suddenly begin to thump again. She looked at Barry, his figure lost in the shadow, only his face dimly visible in the starlight, and some feeling, new, young, terrifying, and yet infinitely delicious, rushed over her. She might have been a girl of seventeen instead of a sober woman fifteen years older, with wifehood, and motherhood, and widowhood all behind her.

"A wonderful night!" said Barry, looking down at the dark mass of tree-tops that almost hid the town, and at the rising circle of shadows that was the hills.

"And a good place to be, Santa Paloma," Sidney added, contentedly. "It's my captured dream, my own home and garden!" With her head resting against one of the pillars of the porch, her eyes dreamily moving from the hills to the sky and over the quiet woods, she went on thoughtfully: "You know I never had a home, Barry; and when I visited here, I began to realize what I was missing. How I longed for Santa Paloma, the creek, and the woods, and my little sunny room after I went away! But even when I was eighteen, and we took a house in Washington, what could I do? I 'came out,' you know. I loved gowns and parties then, as I hope the girls will some day; but I knew all the while it wasn't living." She paused, but Barry did not speak. "And, then, before I was twenty, I was married," Sidney went on presently, "and we started off for St. Petersburg. And after that, for years and years, I posed for dressmakers; I went the round of jewelers, and milliners, and manicures; I wrote notes and paid calls. I let one strange woman come in every day and wash my hands for me, and another wash my hair, and a third dress me! I let men--who were in the business simply to make money, and who knew how to do it!--tell me that my furs must be recut, or changed, and my jewels reset, and my wardrobe restocked and my furniture carried away and replaced. And in the cities we lived in it's horrifying to see how women slave, and toil, and worry to keep up. Half the women I knew were sick over debts and the necessity for more debts. I felt like saying, with Carlyle, 'Your chaos-ships must excuse me'; I'm going back to Santa Paloma, to wear my things as long as they are whole and comfortable, and do what I want to do with my spare time!"

"You missed your playtime," Barry said; "now you make the most of it."

"Oh, no!" she answered, giving him a glimpse of serious eyes in the half-dark, "playtime doesn't come back. But, at least, I know what I want to do, and it will be more fun than any play. One of the wisest men I ever knew set me thinking of these things. He's a sculptor, a great sculptor, and he lives in an olive garden in Italy, and eats what his peasants eat, and befriends them, and stands for their babies in baptism, and sits with them when they're dying. My father and I visited him about two years ago, and one day when he and I were taking a tramp, I suddenly burst out that I envied him. I wanted to live in an olive garden, too, and wear faded blue clothes, and eat grapes, and tramp about the hills. He said very simply that he had worked for twenty years to do it. 'You see, I'm a rich man,' he said, 'and it seems that one must be rich in this world before one dare be poor from choice. I couldn't do this if people didn't know that I could have an apartment in Paris, and servants, and motor-cars, and all the rest of it. It would hurt my daughters and distress my friends. There are hundreds and thousands of unhappy people in the world who can't afford to be poor, and if ever you get a chance, you try it. You'll never be rich again.' So I wrote him about a month ago that I had found MY olive garden," finished Sidney contentedly, "and was enjoying it."

"Captain Burgoyne was older than you, Sid?" Barry questioned. "Wouldn't he have loved this sort of life?"

"Twenty years older, yes; but he wouldn't have lived here for one DAY!" she answered vivaciously. "He was a diplomat, a courtier to his finger-tips. He was born to the atmosphere of hothouse flowers, and salons, and delightful little drawing-room plots and gossip. He loved politics, and power, and women in full dress, and men with orders. Of course I was very new to it all, but he liked to spoil me, draw me out. If it hadn't been for his accident, I never would have grown up at all, I dare say. As it was, I was more like his mother. We went to Washington for the season, New York for the opera, England for autumn visits, Paris for the spring: I loved to make him happy, Barry, and he wasn't happy except when we were going, going, going. He was exceptionally popular; he had exceptional friends, and he couldn't go anywhere without me. My babies were with his mother--"

She paused, turning a white rose between her fingers. "And afterwards," she said presently, "there was Father. And Father never would spend two nights in the same place if he could help it."

"I wasn't drawn back here as you were," said Barry thoughtfully, "I liked New York; I could have made good there if I'd had a chance. It made me sick to give it up, then; but lately I've been feeling differently. A newspaper's a pretty influential thing, wherever it is. I've been thinking about that clubhouse plan of yours; I wish to the Lord that we could do something for those poor kids over there. You're right. Those girls have rotten homes. The whole family gathers in the parlor right after dinner. Pa takes his shoes off, and props his socks up before the stove; Ma begins to hear a kid his spelling; and other kids start the graphophone, and Aggie is expected to ask her young man to walk right in. So after that she meets him in the street, and the girls begin to talk about Aggie."

"Oh, Barry, I'm so glad you're interested!" Standing a step above him, Sidney's ardent face was very close to his own. "Of course we can do it," she said.

"We!" he echoed almost bitterly. "YOU'LL do it; you're the one--" He broke off with a short, embarrassed laugh. "I was going to cut that sort of thing out," he said gruffly, "but all roads lead to Rome, it seems. I can't talk to you five minutes without--and I've got to go. I said I'd look in at the office."

"You seem to be afraid to be friendly lately, Barry," said Mrs. Burgoyne in a hurt voice, flinging away the rose she had been holding, "but don't you think our friendship means something to me, too? I don't like you to talk as if I did all the giving and you all the taking. I don't know how the girls and I would get along without your advice and help here at the Hall. I think," her voice broke into a troubled laugh, "I think you forget that the quality of friendship is not strained."

"Sidney," he said with sudden resolution, turning to face her bravely, "I can't be just friends with you. You're so much the finest, so much the best--" He left the sentence unfinished, and began again: "You have a hundred men friends; you can't realize what you mean to me. You--but you know what you are, and I'm the editor of a mortgaged country paper, a man who has made a mess of things, who can't take care of his kid, or himself, on his job without help--"

"Barry--" she began breathlessly, but he interrupted her.

"Listen to me," he said huskily, taking both her warm hands in his, "I want to tell you something. Say that I WAS weak enough to forget all that, your money and my poverty, your life and my life, everything that puts you as far above me as the moon and stars; say that I could do that--although I hope it's not true--even then--even then I'm not free, Sidney. There is Hetty, you know; there is Billy's mother--"

There was a silence. Sidney slowly freed her hands, laid one upon her heart as unconsciously as a hurt child, and the other upon his shoulder. Her troubled eyes searched his face.

"Barry," she said with a little effort, "have I been mistaken in thinking Billy's mother was dead?"

"Everyone thinks so," he answered with a quick rush of words that showed how great the relief of speech was. "Even up in Hetty's home town, Plumas, they think so. I wrote home that Hetty had left me, and they drew their own conclusions. It was natural enough; she was never strong. She was always restless and unhappy, wanted to go on the stage. She did go on the stage, you know; her mother advised it, and she--just left me. We were in New York, then; Bill was a little shaver; I was having a hard time with a new job. It was an awful time! After a few months I brought Bill back here--he wasn't very well--and then I found that everyone thought Hetty was dead. Then her mother wrote me, and said that Hetty had taken a stage-name, and begged me to let people go on thinking she was dead, and, more for the kid's sake than Hetty's, I let things stand. But Hetty's in California now; she and her mother live in San Francisco; she is still studying singing, I believe. She gets the rent from two flats I have there. But she never writes. And that," he finished grimly, "is the last chapter of my history."

Sidney still stood close to him, earnest, fragrant, lovely, in her white gown. And even above the troubled tumult of his thoughts Barry had time to think how honest, how unaffected she was, to stand so, making no attempt to disguise the confusion in her own mind. For a long time there was no sound but the vague stir of the night about them, the faint breath of some wandering breeze, the rustling flight of some small animal in the dark, the far-hushed, village sounds.

"Thank you, Barry," Sidney said at length. "I'm sorry. I am glad you told me. Good-night."

"Good-night," he said almost inaudibly. He ran down the steps and plunged into the dark avenue without a backward look. Sidney turned slowly, and slowly entered the dimly lighted hall, and shut the door.

CHAPTER XI

"Come down here--we're down by the river!" called Mrs. Burgoyne, from the shade of the river bank, where she and Mrs. Lloyd were busy with their sewing. "The American History section is entertaining the club."

"You look studious!" laughed Mrs. Brown, coming across the grass, to put the Brown baby upon his own sturdy legs from her tired arms, and sink into a deep lawn chair. The June afternoon was warm, but it was delightfully cool by the water. "Is that the club?" she asked, waving toward the group of children who were wading and splashing in the shallows of the loitering river.

"That's the American History Club," responded Mrs. Burgoyne, as she flung her sewing aside and snatched the baby. "Paul," said she, kissing his warm, moist neck, "do you truly love me a little bit?"

"Boy ge' down," said Paul, struggling violently.

"Yes, you shall, darling. But listen, do you want to hear the tick-tock? Oh, Paul, sit still just one minute!"

"Awn ge' DOWN," said Paul, distinctly, every fibre of his small being headed, as it were, for the pebbly shingle where it was daily his delight to dig.

"But say 'deck' first, sweetheart, say 'Deck, I love you,'" besought the mistress of the Hall.

"Deck!" shouted Paul obediently, eyes on the river.

"And a sweet kiss!" further stipulated Mrs. Burgoyne, and grabbed it from his small, red, unresponsive mouth before she let him toddle away. "Yes," she resumed, going on with the tucking of a small skirt, "Joanna and Jeanette and the Adams boy have to write an essay this week about the Battle of Bunker Hill, so I read them Holmes' poem, and they acted it all out. You never saw anything so delicious. Mrs. Lloyd came up just in time to see Mabel limping about as the old Corporal! The cherry tree was the steeple, of course, and both your sons, you'll be ashamed to hear, were redcoats. Next week they expect to do Paul Revere, and I daresay we'll have the entire war, before we're through. You are both cordially invited."

"I'll come," said the doctor's wife, smiling. "I love this garden. And to take care of the boys and have a good time myself is more than I ever thought I'd do in this life!"

"I live on this bank," said Mrs. Burgoyne, leaning back luxuriously in her big chair, to stare idly up through the apple-tree to the blue sky. "I'm going to teach the children all their history and poetry and myths, out here. It makes it so real to them, to act it. Jo and Ellen and I read Barbara Frietchie out here a few weeks ago, and they've wanted it every day or two, since."

"We won't leave anything for the schools to do," said little Mrs. Brown.

"All the better," Mrs. Burgoyne said, cheerfully.

"Well, excuse me!" Mrs. Lloyd, holding the linen cuff she was embroidering at arm's length, and studying it between half-closed lids. "I am only too glad to turn Mabel over to somebody else part of the time. You don't know what she is when she begins to ask questions!"

"I don't know anything more tiring than being with children day in and day out," said Mrs. Brown, "it gets frightfully on your nerves!"

"Oh, I'd like about twelve!" said Mrs. Burgoyne.

"Oh, Mrs. Burgoyne! You WOULDN'T!"

"Yes, I would, granted a moderately secure income, and a rather roomy country home. Although," added Mrs. Burgoyne, temperately, "I do honestly think twelve children is too big a family. However, one may be greedy in wishes!"

"Would you want a child of yours to go without proper advantages," said Mrs. Lloyd, a little severely, "would you want more than one or two, if you honestly felt you couldn't give them all that other children have? Would you be perfectly willing to have your children feel at a disadvantage with all the children of your friends? I wouldn't," she answered herself positively, "I want to do the best by Mabel, I want her to have everything, as she grows up, that a girl ought to have. That's why all this nonsense about the size of the American family makes me so tired! What's the use of bringing a lot of children into the world that are going to suffer all sorts of privations when they get here?"

"Privations wouldn't hurt them," said Mrs. Burgoyne, sturdily, "if it was only a question of patched boots and made-over clothes and plain food. They could even have everything in the world that's worth while."

"How do you mean?" said Mrs. Lloyd, promptly defensive.

"I'd gather them about me," mused Sidney Burgoyne, dreamily, her eyes on the sky, a whimsical smile playing about her mouth, "I'd gather all seven together--"

"Oh, you've come down to seven?" chuckled Mrs. Brown.

"Well, seven's a good Biblical number," Mrs. Burgoyne said serenely, "--and I'd say 'Children, all music is yours, all art is yours, all literature is yours, all history and all philosophy is waiting to prove to you that in starting poor, healthy, and born of intelligent and devoted parents, you have a long head-start in the race of life. All life is ahead of you, friendships, work, play, tramps through the green country in the spring, fires in winter, nights under the summer stars. Choose what you like, and work for it, your father and I can keep you warm and fed through your childhoods, and after that, nothing can stop you if you are willing to work and wait."

"And then suppose your son asks you why he can't go camping with the other boys in summer school, and your daughter wants to join the cotillion?" asked Mrs. Lloyd.

"Why, it wouldn't hurt them to hear me say no," said Mrs. Burgoyne, in surprise. "I never can understand why parents, who practise every imaginable self-denial themselves, are always afraid the first renunciation will kill their child. Sooner or later they are going to learn what life is. I know a little girl whose parents are multi-millionaires, and who is going to be told some day soon that her two older sisters aren't living abroad, as she thinks, but shut up for life, within a few miles of her. What worse blow could life give to the poorest girl?"

"Horrors!" murmured Mrs. Brown.

"And those are common cases," Mrs. Burgoyne said eagerly, "I knew of so many! Pretty little girls at European watering-places whose mothers are spending thousands, and hundreds of thousands of dollars to get out of their blood what no earthly power can do away with. Sons of rich fathers whose valets themselves wouldn't change places with them! And then the fine, clean, industrious middle-classes--or upper classes, really, for the blood in their veins is the finest in the world--are afraid to bring children into the world because of dancing cotillions and motor-cars!"

"Well, of course I have only four," said Mrs. Brown, "but I've been married only seven years--"

Mrs. Burgoyne laughed, came to a full stop, and reddened a little as she went back busily to her sewing.

"Why do you let me run on at such a rate; you know my hobbies now!" she reproached them. "I am not quite sane on the subject of what ought to be done--and isn't--in that good old institution called woman's sphere."

"That sounds vaguely familiar," said Mrs. Lloyd.

"Woman's sphere? Yes, we hate the sound of it," said Mrs. Burgoyne, "just as a man who has left his family hates to talk of home ties, and just as a deserter hates the conversation to come around to the army. But it's true. Our business is children, and kitchens, and husbands, and meals, and we detest it all--"

"I like my husband a little," said Mrs. Brown, in a meek little voice.

They all laughed. Then said Mrs. Lloyd, gazing sentimentally toward the river bank, where her small daughter's twisted curls were tossing madly in a game of "tag":

"I shall henceforth regard Mabel as a possible Joan of Arc."

"One of those boys MAY be a Lincoln, or a Thomas Edison, or a Mark Twain," Sidney Burgoyne added, half-laughing, "and then we'll feel just a little ashamed for having turned him complacently over to a nurse or a boarding school. Of course, it leaves us free to go to the club and hear a paper on the childhood of Napoleon, carefully compiled years after his death. Why, men take heavy chances in their work, they follow up the slightest opening, but we women throw away opportunities to be great, every day of our lives! Scientists and theorists are spending years of their lives pondering over every separate phase of the development of children, but we, who have the actual material in our hands, turn it over to nursemaids!"

"Yes, but lots of children disappoint their parents bitterly," said Mrs. Brown, "and lots of good mothers have bad children!"

"I never knew a good mother to have a bad child--" began Mrs. Burgoyne.

"Well, I have. Thousands," Mrs. Lloyd said promptly.

"Oh, no! Not a BAD child," her hostess said, quickly. "A disappointing child perhaps, or a strong-willed child, you mean. But no good mother--and that doesn't mean merely a good woman, or a church-going woman!--could possibly have a really bad child. 'By their fruits,' you know. And then of course we haven't a perfect system of nursery training yet; we expect angels. We judge by little, inessential things, we're exacting about unimportant trifles. We don't want our sons to marry little fluffy-headed dolls, although the dolls may make them very good wives. We don't want them to make a success of real estate, if the tradition of the house is for the bar or the practice of medicine. And we lose heart at the first suspicion of bad company, or of drinking; although the best men in the world had those temptations to fight! But, anyway, I would rather try at that and fail, than do anything else in the world. My failures at least might save some other woman's children. And it's just that much more done for the world than guarding the valuable life of a Pomeranian, or going to New York for new furs!" They all laughed, for Mrs. Willard White's latest announcement of her plans had awakened some comment among them.

"Mother, am I interrupting you?" said a patient voice at this point. Ellen Burgoyne, rosy, dishevelled, panting, stood some ten feet away, waiting patiently a chance to enter the conversation.

"No, my darling." Her mother held out a welcoming hand. "Oh, I see," she added, glancing at her watch. "It's half-past four. Yes, you can go up for the gingerbread now. You mustn't carry the milk, you know, Ellen."

"Mother," said Ellen, flashing into radiance at the slightest encouragement, "have you told them about our Flower Festibul plans?"

"Oh, not yet!" Mrs. Burgoyne heaved a great sigh. "I'm afraid I've committed myself to an entry for the parade," she told the others ruefully.

"Oh, don't tell me you're going to compete!" exclaimed Mrs. Brown.

"Well, we're rather afraid we are!" Mrs. Burgoyne's voice, if fearful, was hopeful too, for Ellen's face was a study. "Why, is it such a terrible effort?"

"Oh, yes, it's an appalling amount of struggle and fuss, there's all sorts of red tape, and the flowers are so messy," answered the doctor's wife warningly, "and this year will be worse than ever. The Women's Club of Apple Creek is going to enter a carriage, and you know our club is to have the White's motor; it will be perfectly exquisite! It's to be all pink carnations, and Mr. White's nephew, a Berkeley boy, and some of his friends, all in white flannels, are going to run it. Doctor says there'll be a hundred entries this year."

"Well, I'm afraid I'm in for it," said Mrs. Burgoyne, with a sigh. "I haven't the least idea in the world what I'm going to do. It isn't as if we even had a surrey. But I really was involved before I had time to think. You know I've been trying, with some of my spare time," her eyes twinkled, "to get hold of these little factory and cannery girls over in Old Paloma."

"You told me," said Mrs. Brown, "but I don't see how that--"

"Well, you see, their ringleader has been particularly ungracious to me. A fine, superb, big creature she is, named Alice Carter. This Alice came up to the children and me in the street the other day, and told me, in the gruffest manner, that she was interested in a little crippled girl over there, and had promised to take her to see the Flower Festival. But it seems the child's mother was afraid to trust her to Alice in the crowd and heat. Quite simply she asked me if I could manage it. I was tremendously touched, and we went to see the child. She's a poor, brave little scrap--twelve years old, did she say, Baby?"

"Going on thirteen," said Ellen rapidly; "and her father is dead, and her mother works, and she takes care of such a fat baby, and she is very gen-tul with him, isn't she, Mother? And she cried when Mother gave her books, and she can't eat her lunch because her back aches, but she gave the baby his lunch, and Mother asked her if she would let a doctor fix her back, and she said, 'Oh, no!'--didn't she, Mother? She just twisted and twisted her hands, and said, 'I can't.' And Mother said, 'Mary, if you will be a brave girl about the doctor, I will make you a pink dress and a wreath of roses, and you shall ride with the others in the Flower Festibul!' And she just said, 'Oo-oo!'--didn't she, Mother? And she said she thought God sent you, didn't she, Mother?"

"She did." Mrs. Burgoyne smiled through wet lashes. Mrs. Brown wiped her own eyes against the baby's fluffy mop. "She's a most pathetic little creature, this Mary Scott," went on the other woman when Ellen had dashed away, "and I'm afraid she's not the only one. There's my Miss Davids' little sister; if I took her in, Miss Davids would be free for the day; and there's a little deaf-mute whose mother runs the bakery. And I told Mary we'd manage the baby, too, and that if she knew any other children who positively couldn't come any other way, she must let me know. Of course the school children are cared for, they will have seats right near the grand stand, and sing, and so on. But I am really terrified about it, you'll have to help me out."

"I'll do anything," Mrs. Brown promised.

"I'll do anything I CAN," said Mrs. Lloyd, modestly, "I loathe and abominate children unless they're decently dressed and smell of soap--but I'll run a machine, if some one'll see that they don't swarm over me."

"I'll put a barbed wire fence around you!" promised Mrs. Burgoyne, gaily.

Mrs. Carew, coming up, as she expressed it, "to gather up some children," was decidedly optimistic about the plan. "Nobody ever uses hydrangeas, because you can't make artificial ones to fill in with," she said, "so you can get barrels of them." Mrs. Burgoyne was enthusiastic over hydrangeas, "But it's not the fancy touches that scare me," she confessed; "it's the awful practical side."

"What does Barry think?" Mrs. Carew presently asked innocently. Mrs. Burgoyne's suddenly rosy face was not unobserved by any of the others.

"I haven't seen him for several days, not since the night of my dinner," she admitted; "I've been lazy, sending my work down to the office. But I will see him right away."

"He's the one really to have ideas," Mrs. Brown assured her.

CHAPTER XII

So Barry was invited up to the Hall to dinner, and found himself so instantly swept into the plan that he had no time to be self-conscious. Dinner was served on the side porch, and the sunlight filtered across the white cloth, and turned the garden into a place of enchantment. When Billy and the small girls had seized two cookies and two peaches apiece, and retired to the lawn to enjoy them, he and Sidney sat talking on in the pleasant dusk.

"You've asked eight, so far," he said, as she was departing for the office an hour or so after dinner was finished, "but do you think that's all?"

"Oh, it positively must be!" Sidney said virtuously, but there was a wicked gleam in her eye that prepared him for her sudden descent upon the office two days later, with the startling news that now she had positively STOPPED, but fourteen children had been asked!

Barry, rather to her surprise, remained calm.

"Well, I've got an idea," he said presently, "that will make that all right, fourteen children or twenty, it won't make any difference. Only, it may not appeal to you."

"Oh, it will--and you are an angel!" said the lady fervently.

"I've got a friend up the country here in a lumber-mill," Barry explained, "Joe Painter--he hauls logs down from the forest to the river, with a team of eight oxen. Now, if he'd lend them, and you got a hay-wagon from Old Paloma, you wouldn't have any trouble at all."

"Oh, but Barry," she gasped, her face radiant, "would he lend them?"

"I think he would; he'd have to come too, you know, and drive them. I'll ride up and see, anyway."

"Oxen," mused Mrs. Burgoyne, "how perfectly glorious! The children will go wild with joy. And, you see, my Indian boys--"

"Your WHAT?"

"I didn't mention them," said Sidney serenely, "because they'll walk alongside, and won't count in the load. But, you see, some of those nice little mill-boys who don't go to school heard the girls talking about it, and one of them asked me--so wistfully!--if there was anything THEY could do. I immediately thought of Indian costumes."

"But how the deuce will you get the costumes made?" said Barry, drawing a sheet of paper toward him, and beginning some calculations, with an anxious eye.

"Why, it's just cheese-cloth for the girls. Mrs. Brown and I have our machines up in the barn, and Mrs. Carew and Mrs. Adams will come up and help, there's not much to THAT! Barry, if you will really get us this--this ox-man--nothing else will worry me at all."

"You'll have to put the beasts up in your barn."

"Oh, surely! Ask him what they eat. Oh, Barry, we MUST have them! Think how picturesque they'll be! I've been thinking my entry would be a disgrace to the parade, but I don't believe it will be so bad. Barry, when will we know about it?"

"You can count on it, I guess. Joe won't refuse," Barry said, with his lazy smile.

"Oh, you're an angel! I'm going shopping this instant. Barry, there will be room now for my Ellen, and Billy, and Dicky Carew, won't there? It seems their hearts are bursting with the desire. Bunting," murmured Sidney, beginning a list, "cheese-cloth, pink, blue, and cream, bolts of it; twine, beads, leather, feathers; some big white hats; ice-cream, extra milk--"

"Hold on! What for?"

"Why, they have to have something to eat afterward," she reproached him. "We're going to have a picnic up at the Hall. Then those that can will join their people for the fireworks, and the others will be taken home to Old Paloma. The little Scott girl will stay with Ellen and Jo overnight; Mammy Currey will look after them, and they'll watch the fireworks from my porch. I've written to ask Doctor Young--he's the best in San Francisco--to come up from the city next day to see what he thinks can be done for Mary Scott."

"You get a lot of fun out of your money, don't you, Sidney?" said Barry, watching her amusedly, as she tucked the list into her purse and arose with a great air of business.

"More than any one woman deserves," she answered soberly.

"Walter," said Anne Pratt to her brother, one evening about this time, as she decorously filled his plate from the silver tureen, "have you heard that Mrs. Burgoyne has gathered up about twenty children in Old Paloma--cripples, and orphans, and I don't know what all!--and is getting up a wagon for the Flower Festival? I was up at the Hall to-day, and they're working like beavers."

"Carew said something about it," said Walter Pratt. "Seems a good idea. Those poor little kids over there don't have much fun."

"You never said so before, Walter," his sister returned almost resentfully.

"I don't know why I shouldn't have," said Walter literally. "It's true."

"If we did anything for any children, it ought to be Lizzie's," said Miss Pratt uncomfortably, after a pause.

"I wish to the Lord we COULD do something for Lizzie's kids," her brother observed suddenly. "I suppose it would kill you to have 'em up here?"

"Kill me!" Miss Anne echoed with painful eagerness, and with a sudden tremble of her thin, long hand. "I don't know why it should; there never were better behaved children born. I don't like Lizzie's husband, and never shall;" she rushed on, "but seeing those children up at the Hall to-day made me think of Betty, and Hope, and Davy, cooped up down there in town. They'd love the Flower Festival, and I could take them up to the Hall, and Nanny would be wild with joy to have Lizzie's children here; she'd bake cookies and gingerbread--" A flush had come into her faded, cool cheek. "Wouldn't they be in your way? You really wouldn't mind--you won't change your mind about it, Walt?" she said timidly.

"Change my mind! Why, I'll love to have them running round here," he answered warmly. "Write Lizzie to-night, and tell her I've got to go down Tuesday, and I'll bring 'em up."

"I'll tell her that just the things they have will be quite good enough," said Miss Pratt. "The Burgoyne children just wear play-ginghams--I'll get them anything else they need!"

"It won't interfere with your club work, Anne?"

"Not in the least!" She was sure of that, "And anyway," she went on decidedly, "I'm not going to the club so much this summer. Mary Brown and I went yesterday, and there was--well, I suppose it was a good paper on 'The Mind of the Child,' by Miss Sarah Rich. But it seemed so flat. And Mary Brown said, coming away, 'I think Doctor and I will still come to the monthly receptions, but I believe I won't listen to any more papers like that. They're all very well for people who have no children--'"

"Well, by Tuesday night you'll have three!" said Walter, with what was for him great gaiety of manner.

"Walter," his sister suggested nervously, "you'll be awfully affectionate with Lizzie, won't you? Be sure to tell her that we WANT them; and tell her that they'll be playing up at the Hall all summer, as we used to. You know, I've been thinking, Walter," went on the poor lady, with her nose suddenly growing red and her eyes watering, "that I've not been a very good sister to Lizzie. She's the youngest, and Mother--Mother wasn't here to advise her about her marriage, and--and now I don't write her; and she wrote me that Betty had a cough, and Davy was so noisy indoors in wet weather--and I just go to the Club to hear papers upon 'Napoleon' and 'The Mind of the Child.'" And Miss Anne, beginning to cry outright, leaned back in her chair, and covered her face with her handkerchief.

"Well, Anne--well, Anne," her brother said huskily, "we'll make it up now. Where are you going to put them?" he presently added, with an inspiration.

Miss Pratt straightened up, blew her nose, wiped her eyes, and rang for the maid.

"Betty and Hope in the big front room--" she began happily.

Another brief conversation, this time between George Carew and his wife, was indicative of a certain change of view-point that was affecting the women of Santa Paloma in these days. Mr. Carew, coming home one evening, found a very demure and charming figure seated on the porch. Mrs. Carew's gown was simplicity itself: a thin, dotted, dark blue silk, with a deep childish lace collar and cuffs.

"You look terribly sweet, Jen," said Mr. Carew; "you look out of sight." And when he came downstairs again, and they were at dinner, he returned to the subject with, "Jen, I haven't seen you look so sweet for a long time. What is that, a new dress? Is that for the reception on the Fourth? Jen, didn't you have a dress like that when we were first married?"

"Sorrel made this, and it only cost sixty dollars," said Mrs. Carew.

"Well, get her to make you another," her husband said approvingly. At which Mrs. Carew laughed a little shakily, and came around the table, and put her arms about him and said:

"Oh, George, you dear old BAT! Miss Pomeroy made this, upstairs here, in three days, and the silk cost nine dollars. I DID have a dress like this in my trousseau--my first silk--and I thought it was wonderful; and I think you're a darling to remember it; and I AM going to wear this on the Fourth. It's nice enough, isn't it?"

"Nice enough! You'll be the prettiest woman there," stated Mr. Carew positively.

CHAPTER XIII

The earliest daylight of July Fourth found Santa Paloma already astir. Dew was heavy on the ropes of flowers and greens, and the flags and bunting that made brilliant all the line of the day's march; and long scarfs of fog lingered on the hills, but for all that, and despite the delicious fragrant chill of the morning air, nobody doubted that the day would be hot and cloudless, and the evening perfect for fireworks. Lawn-sprinklers began to whir busily in the sweet shaded gardens long before the sunlight reached them; windows and doors were flung open to the air; women, sweeping garden-paths and sidewalks with gay energy, called greetings up and down the street to one another. Chairs were dragged out-of-doors; limp flags began to stir in the sunny air; other flags squeakily mounted their poles. At every window bunting showed; the schoolhouse was half-hidden in red, white, and blue; the women's clubhouse was festooned with evergreens and Japanese lanterns; and the Mail office, the grand stand opposite, the shops, and the bank, all fluttered with gay colors. Children shouted and scampered everywhere; gathered in fascinated groups about the ice-cream and candy and popcorn booths that sprang up at every corner; met arriving cousins and aunts at the train; ran on last-minute errands. Occasionally a whole package of exploding firecrackers smote the warm still air.

By half-past ten every window on the line of march, every dooryard and porch, had its group of watchers. Wagons and motor-cars, from the surrounding villages and ranches, blocked the side streets. It was very warm, and fans and lemonade had a lively sale.

From the two available windows of the Mail office, three persons, as eager as the most eager child, watched the gathering crowds, and waited for the Flower Parade. They were Mrs. Apostleman, stately in black lace, and regally fanning, Sidney Burgoyne, looking her very prettiest in crisp white, with a scarlet scarf over her arm, and Barry Valentine, who looked unusually festive himself in white flannels. All three were in wild spirits.

"Hark, here they come!" said Sidney at last, drawing her head in from a long inspection of the street. She had been waving and calling greetings in every direction for a pleasant half-hour. Now eleven had boomed from the town-hall clock, and a general restlessness and wiltedness began to affect the waiting crowds.

Barry immediately dangled almost his entire length across the window sill, and screwed his person about for a look.

"H'yar dey come, li'l miss, sho's yo' bawn!" he announced joyfully. "There's the band!"

Here they came, sure enough, under the flags and garlands, through the noonday heat. Only vague brassy notes and the general craning of necks indicated their approach now; but in another five minutes the uniformed band was actually in view, and the National Guard after it, tremendously popular, and the Native Sons, with another band, and the veterans, thin, silver-headed old men in half a dozen carriages, and more open carriages. One held the Governor and his wife, the former bowing and smiling right and left, and saluted by the rising school children, when he seated himself in the judges' stand, with the shrill, thrilling notes of the national anthem.

And then another band, and--at last!--the slow-moving, flower-covered carriages and motors, a long, wonderful, brilliant line of them. White-clad children in rose-smothered pony-carts, pretty girls in a setting of scarlet carnations, more pretty girls half-hidden in bobbing and nodding daisies--every one more charming than the last. There were white horses as dazzling as soap and powder could make them; horses whose black flanks glistened as dark as coal, and there was a tandem of cream-colored horses that tossed rosettes of pink Shirley poppies in their ears. The Whites' motor-car, covered with pink carnations, and filled with good-looking lads flying the colors of the Women's Club and the nation's flag, won a special round of applause. Mrs. Burgoyne and Barry loyally clapped for the Pratt motor-car, from which Joanna Burgoyne and Lizzie Pratt's children were beaming upon the world.

"But what are they halting for, and what are they clapping?" Sidney presently demanded, when a break in the line and a sudden outburst of cheering and applause interrupted the parade. Barry again hung at a dangerous angle from the window. Presently he sat back, his face one broad smile.

"It's us," he remarked simply. "Wait until you see us; we're the cream of the whole show!"

Too excited to speak, Sidney knelt breathless at the sill, her eyes fixed upon the spot where the cause of the excitement must appear. She was perhaps the only one of all the watchers who did not applaud, as the eight powerful oxen came slowly down the sunshiny street, guided by the tall, lean driver who walked beside them, and dragging the great wagon and its freight of rapturous children.

Only an old hay-wagon, after all; only a team of shabby oxen, such as a thousand lumber-camps in California might supply; only a score or more of the ill-nourished, untrained children of the very poor; but what an enchantment of love and hope and summer-time had been flung over them all! The body of the wagon was entirely hidden by exquisite hydrangeas; the wheels were moving disks of the pale pink and blue blossoms; the oxen, their horns gilded, their polished hoofs twinkling as they moved, wore yokes that seemed solidly made of the flowers, and great ropes of blossoms hid the swinging chains. Over each animal a brilliant cover had been flung; and at the head of each a young Indian boy, magnificent in wampum and fringed leather, feathers and beads, walked sedately. The children were grouped, pyramid-fashion, on the wagon, in a nest of hydrangea blooms, the pink, and cream, and blue of their gowns blending with the flowers all about them, the sunlight shining full in their happy eyes. Over their shoulders were garlands of poppies, roses, sweet-peas, daisies, carnations, lilies, or other blossoms; their hands were full of flowers. But it was the radiance of their faces that shone brightest, after all. It was the little consumptive's ecstatic smile, as she sat resting against an invisible support; it was the joy in Mary Scott's thin eager face, framed now in her loosened dark hair, and with the shadow, like her crutch, laid aside for a while, that somehow brought tears to the eyes that watched. Santa Paloma cheered and applauded these forgotten children of hers; and the children laughed and waved their hands in return.

Youth and happiness and summer-time incarnate, the vision went on its way, down the bright street; and other carriages followed it, and were praised as those that had gone before had been. But no entry in any flower parade that Santa Paloma had ever known, was as much discussed as this one. Indeed, it began a new era; but that was later on. When Mrs. Burgoyne's plain white frock appeared among the elaborate gowns worn at the club luncheon that afternoon, she was quite overwhelmed by congratulations. She went away very early, to superintend the children's luncheon at the Hall, and then Mrs. White had a chance to tell the distinguished guests who she was, and that she could well afford to play Lady Bountiful to the Santa Paloma children.

"One wouldn't imagine it, she seems absolutely simple and unspoiled," said Mrs. Governor.

"She is!" said Mrs. Lloyd unexpectedly.

"I told her how scared most of us had been at the mere idea of her coming here, Parker," Mrs. Lloyd told her husband later, "and how friendly she is, and that she always wears little wash dresses, and that the other girls are beginning to wear checked aprons and things, because her girls do! Of course, I said it sort of laughingly, you know, but I don't think Clara White liked it ONE BIT, and I don't care! Clara is rather mad at me, anyway," she went on, musingly, "because yesterday she telephoned that she was going to send that Armenian peddler over here, with some Madeira lunch cloths. They WERE beauties, and only twenty-three dollars; you'd pay fifty for them at Raphael Weil's--they're smuggled, I suppose! But I simply said, 'Clara, I can't afford it!' and let it go at that. She laughed--quite cattily, Parker!--and said, 'Oh, that's rather funny!' But I don't care whether Clara White thinks I'm copying Mrs. Burgoyne or not! I might as well copy her as somebody else!"

Mrs. Burgoyne and Barry Valentine went down-town on the evening of the great day, to see the fireworks and the crowds, and to hear the announcements of prize-winners. Santa Paloma was in holiday mood, and the two entered into the spirit of the hour like irresponsible children. It was a warm, wonderful summer night; the sky was close and thickly spangled with stars. Main Street bobbed with Japanese lanterns, rang with happy voices and laughter. The jostling, pushing currents of men in summer suits, and joyous girls in thin gowns, were all good-natured. Sidney found friends on all sides, and laughed and called her greetings as gaily as anyone.

Barry had a rare opportunity to watch her unobserved, as she went her happy way; the earnest happy brightness in her eyes, when some shabby little woman from Old Paloma laid a timid hand on her arm, her adoring interest in the fat babies that slumbered heavily on paternal shoulders, her ready use of names, "Isn't this fun, Agnes?"--"You haven't lost Harry, have you, Mrs. O'Brien?"--"Don't you and your friend want to come and have some ice-cream with us, Josie?"

"But we mustn't waste too much time here, Barry," she would say now and then; for at eight o'clock a "grand concert program and distribution of prizes" was scheduled to take place at the town hall, and Sidney was anxious not to miss an instant of it. "Don't worry, I'll get you there!" Barry would answer reassuringly, amused at her eagerness.

And true to his word, he stopped her at the wide doorway of the concert hall, fully five minutes before the hour, and they found themselves joining the slow stream of men and women and children that was pouring up the wide, dingy stairway. Everyone was trying, in all good humor, to press ahead of everyone else, inspired with the sudden agonizing conviction that in the next two minutes every desirable seat would certainly be gone. Even Sidney, familiar as she was with every grand opera house in the world, felt the infection, and asked rather nervously if any of the seats were reserved.

"Don't worry; we'll get seats," said the imperturbable Barry, and several children in their neighborhood laughed out in sudden exquisite relief.

Seats indeed there were, although the front rows were filling fast, and all the aisle-chairs were taken by squirming, restless small children. Mrs. Burgoyne sat down, and studied the hall with delighted eyes. It was ordinarily only a shabby, enormous, high-ceiled room, filled with rows of chairs, and with an elevated stage at the far end. But, like all Santa Paloma, it was in holiday trim to-night. All the windows--wide open to the summer darkness--were framed in bunting and drooping flowers, and on the stage were potted palms and crossed flags. Great masses of bamboo and California ferns were tied with red, white and blue streamers between the windows, and, beside these decorations, which were new for the occasion, were purple and yellow banners, left from the night of the Native Sons' Grand Ball and Reception, a month ago, and, arched above the stage the single word "Welcome" in letters two feet high, which dated back to the Ladies of Saint Rose's Parish Annual Fair and Entertainment, in May. If the combined effect of these was not wholly artistic, at least it was very gay, and the murmur of voices and laughter all over the hall was gay, too, and gay almost to intoxication it was to hear the musicians tentatively and subduedly trying their instruments up by the piano, with their sleek heads close together.

Presently every chair in the house had its occupant, and the younger element began a spasmodic sort of clapping, as a delicate hint to the agitated managers, who were behind the scenes, running blindly about with worn scraps of scribbled paper in their hands, desperately attempting to call the roll of their performers. When Joe, the janitor, came out onto the stage, he was royally applauded, although he did no more than move a tin stand on which there were numbered cards, from one side of the stage to the other, and change the number in view from "18" to "1."

Fathers and mothers, perspiring, clean and good-natured, smiled upon youthful impatience and impertinence to-night, as they sat fanning and discussing the newcomers, or leaned forward or backward for hilarious scraps of conversation with their neighbors. Lovers, as always oblivious of time, sat entirely indifferent to the rise or fall of the curtain, the girls with demurely dropped lashes, the men deep in low monotones, their faces close to the lovely faces so near, their arms flung, in all absent-mindedness, across the backs of the ladies' chairs. And any motherly heart might have been stirred with an aching sort of tenderness, as Sidney Burgoyne's was, at the sight of so much awkward, budding manliness, so many shining pompadours, and carefully polished shoes and outrageous cravats--so many silky, filleted little heads, and innocent young bosoms half-hidden by all sorts of dainty little conspiracies of lace and lawn. Youth, enchanting, self-absorbed, important, had coolly taken possession of the hall, as it does of everything, for its own happy plans, and something of the gossamer beauty of it seemed to be clouding older and wiser eyes to-night. Sidney found her eyes resting upon Barry's big, shapely hand, as he leaned forward, deep in conversation with Dr. Brown, in the chair ahead, and she was conscious that she wanted to sit back and shut her eyes, and draw a deep breath of sheer irrational happiness because this WAS Barry next to her, and that he liked to be there.

Presently the hall thrilled to see two modest-looking and obviously embarrassed men come out to seat themselves in the half-circle of chairs that lined the stage, and a moment later applause broke out for the Mayor and his wife, and the members of the Flower Parade Committee of Arrangements, and for the nondescript persons who invariably fill in such a group, and for the kindly, smiling Governor, and the ladies of his party, and for the Willard Whites, who, with the easiest manners in the world, were in actual conversation with the great people as they came upon the stage.

At the sight of them, Mrs. Carew, still vigorously clapping, leaned over to say to Mrs. Burgoyne:

"Look at Clara White! And we were wondering why they didn't come in! Wouldn't she make you TIRED!"

"You might kiss her hand, when you go up to get your prize, Mrs. Burgoyne," suggested Barry, and a general giggle went the rounds.

"If I get a prize," said Sidney, in alarm, "you've got to go up, I couldn't!"

"We'll see--" Barry began, his voice drowned by the opening crash of the band.

There followed what the three papers of Santa Paloma were unanimous the next day in describing as the most brilliant and enjoyable concert ever given in Santa Paloma. It was received with immense enthusiasm, entirely unaffected by the fact that everyone present had heard Miss Emelie Jeanne Foster sing "Twickenham Ferry" before, with "Dawn" as an encore, and was familiar also with the selections of the Stringed Instrument Club, and had listened to young Doctor Perry's impassioned tenor many times. As for George O'Connor, with his irresistible laughing song, and the song about the train that went to Morro to-day, he was more popular every time he appeared, and was greeted now by mad applause, and shouts of "There's George!" and "Hello, George!"

And the Home Boys' Quartette from Emville was quite new, and various solo singers and a "lady elocutionist" from San Francisco were heard for the first time. The latter, who was on the program merely for a "Recitation--Selected," was so successful with "Pauline Pavlovna," and "Seein' Things at Night" that it was nearly ten o'clock before the Governor was introduced.

However, he was at last duly presented to the applauding hundreds, and came forward to the footlights to address them, and made everyone laugh and feel friendly by saying immediately that he knew they hadn't come out that evening to hear an old man make a long speech.

He said he didn't believe in speechmaking much, he believed in DOING things; there were always a lot of people to stand around and make speeches, like himself--and there was more laughter.

He said that he knew the business of the evening was the giving out of these prizes here--he didn't know what was in these boxes--he indicated the daintily wrapped and tied packages that stood on the little table in the middle of the stage--but he thought every lady in the hall would know before she went home, and perhaps some one of them would tell him--and there was more laughter. He said he hoped that there was something mighty nice in the largest box, because he understood that it was to go to a fairy-godmother; he didn't know whether the good people in the hall believed in fairies or not, but he knew that some of the children in Old Paloma did, and he had seen and heard enough that day to make him believe in 'em too! He'd heard of a fairy years ago who made a coach-and-four out of a pumpkin, but he didn't think that was any harder than to make a coach-and-six out of a hay-wagon, and put twenty Cinderellas into it instead of one. He said it gave him great

pride and pleasure to announce that the first prize for to-day's
beautiful contest had been unanimously awarded to--

Sidney Burgoyne, watching him with fascinated eyes, her breath coming
fast and unevenly, her color brightening and fading, heard only so
much, and then, with a desperate impulse to get away, half rose to her
feet.

But she was too late. Long before the Governor reached her name, a
sudden outburst of laughter and clapping shook the hall, there was a
friendly stir and murmur about her; a hundred voices came to her ears,
"It's Mrs. Burgoyne, of course!--She's got it! She's got the first
prize!--Go on up, Mrs. Burgoyne! You've got it!--Isn't that
GREAT,--she's got it! Go up and get it!"

"You've got first prize, I guess. You'll have to go up for it," Barry
urged her.

"He didn't say so!" Sidney protested nervously. But she let herself be
half-pushed into the aisle, and somehow reached the three little steps
that led up to the platform, and found herself facing His Excellency,
in an uproar of applause.

The Governor said a few smiling words as he put a large box into her
hands; Sidney knew this because she saw his lips move, but the house
had gone quite mad by this time, and not a word was audible. Everyone
in the hall knew that a tall loving-cup was in the box, for it had been
on exhibition in the window of Postag's jewelry store for three weeks.
It was of silver, and lined with gold, both metals shining with an
unearthly and flawless radiance; and there was "Awarded--as a First
Prize--in the Twelfth Floral Parade--of Santa Paloma, California" cut
beautifully into one side, and a scroll all ready, on the other side,
to be engraved with the lucky winner's name.

She had been joking for two or three weeks about the possibility of this very occurrence, had been half-expecting it all day, but now suddenly all the joke seemed gone out of it, and she was only curiously stirred and shaken. She looked confusedly down at the sea of faces below her, smiles were everywhere, the eyes that were upon her were full of all affection and pride--She had done so little after all, she said to herself, with sudden humility, almost with shame. And it was so poignantly sweet to realize that they loved her, that she was one of themselves, they were glad she had won, she who had been a stranger to all of them only a few months ago!

Her eyes full of sudden tears, her lip shaking, she could only bow and bow again, and then, just as her smile threatened to become entirely eclipsed, she managed a husky "Thank you all so much!" and descended the steps rapidly, to slip into her chair between Barry and George Carew.

"You know, you oughtn't to make a long tedious speech like that on an occasion like this, Sid," Barry said, when she had somewhat recovered her equilibrium, and the silver loving cup was unwrapped, and was being passed admiringly from hand to hand.

"Don't!" she said warningly, "or you'll have me weeping on your shoulder!"

Instead of which she was her gayest self, and accepted endless congratulations with joyous composure, as the audience streamed out into the reviving festivity of Main Street. The tide was turning in one direction now, for there were to be "fireworks and a stupendous band concert" immediately following the concert, in a vacant lot not far away.

And presently they all found themselves seated on the fragrant grass, under the stars. George Carew, at Sidney's feet, solemnly wrapped sections of molasses popcorn in oiled paper, and passed them to the ladies. Barry's coat made a comfortable seat for Mrs. Burgoyne and little Mrs. Brown; Barry himself was just behind, and Mrs. Carew and her big son beside them. All about, in the darkness, were other groups: mothers and fathers and alert, chattering children. Alice Carter, the big mill-girl, radiant now, and with a hoarse, inarticulate, adoring young plumber in tow, went by them, and stooped to whisper something to Mrs. Burgoyne. "I wish you WOULD come, Alice!" the lady answered eagerly, as they went on.

Then the rockets began to hiss up toward the stars, each falling shower of light greeted with a long rapturous "Ah-h-h!" Catherine-wheels sputtered nearer the ground; red lights made eerie great spots of illumination here and there, against which dark little figures moved.

"I don't know that I ever had a happier day in my life!" said Sidney Burgoyne.

CHAPTER XIV

More happy days followed; for Santa Paloma, after the Fourth of July, felt only friendliness for the new owner of the Hall, and Mrs. Burgoyne's informal teas on the river bank began to prove a powerful attraction, even rivaling the club in feminine favor. Sometimes the hostess enlisted all their sympathies for a newly arrived Old Paloma baby, and they tore lengths of flannel, and busily stitched at tiny garments, under the shade of the willow and pepper trees. Sometimes she had in her care one or more older babies whose busy mother was taking a

day's rest, or whose father was perhaps ill, needing all the wife's
care. Always there was something to read and discuss; an editorial in
some eastern magazine that made them all indignant or enthusiastic, or
a short story worth reading aloud. And almost always the children were
within call, digging great holes in the pebbly shallows of the river,
only to fill them up again, toiling over bridges and dams, climbing out
to the perilous length of the branches that hung above the water.
Little Mary Scott, released from the fear of an "op'ration," and facing
all unconsciously a far longer journey than the dreaded one to a San
Francisco hospital, had her own cushioned chair near the bank, where
she could hear and see, and laugh at everything that went on, and revel
in consolation and bandages when the inevitable accidents made them
necessary. Mary had no cares now, no responsibility more serious than
to be sure her feet didn't get cold, and to tell Mrs. Burgoyne the
minute her head ached; there was to be nothing but rest and comfort and
laughter for her in life now. "I don't know why we should pity her,"
little Mrs. Brown said thoughtfully, one day, as they watched her with
the other children; "we can't ever hope to feel that any of our
children are as safe as she is."

Mrs. Burgoyne's method of entertaining the children was simple. She
always made them work as hard as possible. One day they begged her to
let them build a "truly dam" that would really stop the Lobos in its
placid course. She consulted gravely with George Carew: should they
attempt it? George, after serious consideration, thought they should.

As a result, twenty children panted and toiled through a warm Saturday
afternoon, George and the Adams boys shouting directions as they
handled planks and stones; everybody wet, happy, and excited. Not the
least glorious moment was when the dam was broken at five o'clock, just
before refreshments were served.

"We'll do that better next Saturday," said George. But a week later they wanted to clean the barn and organize a club. Mrs. Burgoyne was sure they couldn't. All that space, she said, and those bins, and the little rooms, and all? Very well, then, they could try. Later they longed for a picnic supper in the woods, with an open fire, and potatoes, and singing. Their hostess was dubious: entreated them to consider the WORK involved, dragging stones for the fire, and carrying potatoes and bacon and jam and all the rest of it 'way up there'. This was at two o'clock, and at six she was formally asked to come up and inspect the cleared camping ground, and the fireplace with its broilers, and the mammoth stack of fuel prepared.

"I knew you'd do it!" said the lady delightedly. "Now we'll really have a fine supper!" And a memorable supper they had, and Indian stories, and singing, and they went home well after dusk, to end the day perfectly.

"They like this sort of thing much better than white dresses, and a professional entertainer, and dancing, and too much ice-cream," said Mrs. Burgoyne to Mrs. Adams.

"Of course they do," said Mrs. Adams, who had her own reasons for turning rather red and speaking somewhat faintly. "And it's much less work, and much less expense," she added.

"Now it is, when they can be out-of-doors," said Mrs. Burgoyne; "but in winter they do make awful work indoors. However, there is tramping for dry weather, and I mean to have a stove set up in the old billiard-room down-stairs and turn them all loose in there when it's wet. Theatricals, and pasting things, and singing, and now and then candy-making, is all fun. And one knows that they're safe, and piling up happy memories of their home."

"You make a sort of profession of motherhood," said Mrs. White dryly.

"It IS my profession," said the hostess, with her happy laugh.

But her happiness had a sudden check in mid-August; Sidney found herself no more immune from heartache than any other woman, no more philosophical over a hurt. It was, she told herself, only a trifle, after all. She was absurd to let it cloud the bright day for her and keep her restless and wakeful at night. It was nothing. Only--

Only it was the first time that Barry had failed her. He was gone. Gone without a word of explanation to anyone, leaving his work at the Mail unfinished, leaving even Billy, his usual confidant, quite in the dark. Sidney had noticed for days a certain moodiness and unresponsiveness about him; had tried rather timidly to win him from it; had got up uneasily half a dozen times in the night just past to look across the garden to his house, and wonder why Barry's light burned on and on.

She had meant to send for him in the morning, but Billy, artlessly appearing when the waffles came on at breakfast, remarked that Dad was gone to San Francisco.

"To the city, Billy?" Sidney asked. "Didn't he say why?"

"He didn't even say goodbye," Billy replied cheerfully. "He just left a note for Hayashi. It said he didn't know how long he would be gone."

Sidney tried with small success to deceive herself into thinking that it was the mere mysteriousness of this that cut her. She presently went down to see Mrs. Carew, and was fretted because that lady would for some time discuss nothing but the successful treatment of insects on the rose-bushes.

"Barry seems to have disappeared," said Sidney finally, in a casual tone.

Mrs. Carew straightened up, forgot hellebore and tobacco juice for the moment.

"Did I tell you what Silva told me?" she asked.

"Silva?" echoed Sidney, at a loss.

"The milkman. He told me that when he came up at five o'clock this morning, Barry came out of the gate, and that he looked AWFULLY. He said he was pale, and that his eyes looked badly, and that he hardly seemed to know what he was doing. And oh, my dear, I'm afraid that he's drinking again! I'm sure of it. It's two years now since he has done this. I think it's too bad. But you know he used to go down to town every little while for a regular TIME with those newspaper men. He doesn't like Santa Paloma, you know. He gets very bored here. He'll be back in a day or two, thoroughly ashamed of himself."

Sidney did not answer, because she could not. Resentment and loyalty, shame and heartache, kept her lips dumb. She walked to and fro in the garden, alone in the sweet early darkness, for an hour. Then she went indoors, and tried to amuse herself at the piano. Suddenly her face twisted, she laid her arm along the rack, and her face on her arm; but it was only for a moment; then she straightened up resolutely, piled the music, closed the piano, and went upstairs.

"But perhaps I'm not old enough yet for an olive garden," she told the stars from her window an hour later.

CHAPTER XV

Another day went by, and still there was no news from Barry. The early autumn weather was exquisite, and Sidney, with the additional work for the Mail that the editor's absence left for her, found herself very busy. But life seemed suddenly to taste flat and uninteresting to her. The sunlight was glaring, the afternoons dusty and windy, and under all the day's duties and pleasures--the meeting of neighbors, the children's confidences, her busy coming and going up and down the village streets--ran a sick undercurrent of disappointment and heartache. She went to the post-office twice, in that first long day, for the arriving mail, and Miss Potter, pleased at these glimpses of the lady from the Hall, chatted blithely as she pushed Italian letters, London letters, letters from Washington and New York, through the little wicket.

But there was not a line from Barry. On the second day Sidney began to think of sending him a note; it might be chanced to the Bohemian Club--

But no, she wouldn't do that. If he did not care enough to write her, she certainly wouldn't write him.

She began to realize how different Santa Paloma was without his big figure, his laughter, his joyous comment upon people and things. She had taken his comradeship for granted, taken it as just one more element of the old childish days regained, never thought of its rude interruption or ending.

Now she felt ashamed and sore, she had been playing with fire, she told herself severely; she had perhaps hurt him; she had certainly given herself needless heartache. No romantic girl of seventeen ever suffered a more unreasoning pang than did Sidney when she came upon Barry's shabby, tobacco-scented office coat, hanging behind his desk, or found in her own desk one of the careless notes he so frequently used to leave there at night for her to find in the morning.

However, in the curious way that things utterly unrelated sometimes play upon each other in this life, these days of bewilderment and chagrin bore certain good fruit. Sidney had for some weeks been planning an attack upon the sympathies of the Santa Paloma Women's Club, but had shrunk from beginning it, because life was running very smoothly and happily, and she was growing too genuinely fond of her new neighbors to risk jeopardizing their affection for her by a move she suspected would be unpopular.

But now she was unhappy, and, with the curious stoicism that is born of unhappiness, she plunged straight into the matter. On the third day after Barry's disappearance she appeared at the regular meeting of the club as Mrs. Carew's guest.

"I hope this means that you are coming to your senses, ye bad girl!" said Mrs. Apostleman, drawing her to the next chair with a fat imperative hand.

"Perhaps it does," Sidney answered, with a rather nervous smile. She sat attentive and appreciative, through the reading of a paper entitled "Some Glimpses of the Real Burns," and seemed immensely to enjoy the four songs--Burns's poems set to music--and the clever recitation of several selections from Burns that followed.

Then the chairman announced that Mrs. Burgoyne, "whom I'm sure we all know, although she isn't one of us yet (laughter), has asked permission to address the club at the conclusion of the regular program." There was a little applause, and Sidney, very rosy, walked rapidly forward, to stand just below the platform. She was nervous, obviously, and spoke hurriedly and in a rather unnatural voice.

"Your chairman and president," she began, with a little inclination toward each, "have given me permission to speak to you today for five minutes, because I want to ask the Santa Paloma Women's Club a favor--a great favor, in fact. I won't say how much I hope the club will decide to grant it, but just tell you what it is. It has to do with the factory girls across the river. I've become interested in some of them; partly I suppose because some friends of mine are working for just such girls, only under infinitely harder circumstances, in some of the eastern cities, I feel, we all feel, I know, that the atmosphere of Old Paloma is a dangerous one for girls. Every year certain ones among them 'go wrong,' as the expression is; and when a girl once does that, she is apt to go very wrong indeed before she stops. She doesn't care what she does, in fact, and her own people only make it harder, practically drive her away. Or even if she marries decently, and tries to live down all the past it comes up between her and her neighbors, between her and her children, perhaps, and embitters her whole life. And so finally she goes to join that terrible army of women that we others try to pretend we never see or hear of at all. These girls work hard all day, and their homes aren't the right sort of homes, with hot dirty rooms,--full of quarreling and crowding; and so they slip out at night and meet their friends in the dancehalls, and the moving-picture shows. And we--we can't blame them." Her voice had grown less diffident, and rang with sudden longing and appeal. "They want only what we all wanted a few years ago," she said. "They want good times, lights and music, and pretty gowns, something to look forward to in the long, hot afternoons--dances, theatricals, harmless meetings of all sorts. If we could give them safe clean fun--not patronizingly, and not too obviously instructive--they'd be willing to wait for it; they'd talk about it instead of more dangerous things; they'd give up dangerous things for it. They are very nice girls, some of them, and their friends are very nice fellows, for the most part, and they are--they are so very young.

"However, about the club--I am wondering if it could be borrowed for a temporary meeting-place for them, if we form a sort of club among them. I say temporary, because I hope we will build them a clubhouse of their own some day. But meantime there is only the Grand Opera House, which all the traveling theatrical companies rent; Hansen's Hall, which is over a saloon, so that won't do; and the Concert Hall, which costs twenty-five dollars a night. We would, of course, see that the club was cleaned after every meeting, and pay for the lights. I--I think that's about all," finished Sidney, feeling that she had put her case rather ineloquently, and coming to a full stop. She sat down, her eyes nowhere, her cheeks very red.

There was the silence of utter surprise in the room. After a pause, Mrs. White raised a gloved hand. Permission from the chair was given Mrs. White to speak.

"Your idea would be to give the Old Paloma girls a dance here, Mrs. Burgoyne?"

"Regular dances, yes," said Sidney, standing up. "To let them use the clubhouse, say, two nights a week. Reading, and singing, and sewing one night, perhaps, and a dance another. Or we could get good moving-picture films, or have a concert or play, and ask the mothers and fathers now and then; charades and Morris dances, something like that."

"Dancing and moving-pictures--oh, dear, dear!" said Mrs. White, with a whimsical smile and a shake of her head, and there was laughter.

"All those things take costuming, and that takes money," said the chairman, after a silence, rather hesitatingly.

"Money isn't the problem," Mrs. Burgoyne rejoined eagerly; "you'll find that they spend a good deal now, even for the wretched pleasures they have."

There was another silence. Then Mrs. White again gained permission to speak, and rose to do so.

"I think perhaps Mrs. Burgoyne, being a newcomer here, doesn't quite understand our feeling toward our little club," she said very pleasantly. "We built it," she went on, with a slight touch of emotion, "as a little refuge from everything jarring and unpleasant; we meant it to stand for something a little BETTER and FINER than the things of everyday life can possibly be. Perhaps we felt that there are already too many dances and too many moving-picture shows in the world; perhaps we felt that if we COULD forget those things for a little while--I don't mean," said Mrs. White smilingly reasonable, "that the reform of wayward girls isn't a splendid and ennobling thing; I believe heartily in the work institutions and schools are doing along those lines, but--" and with a pretty little gesture of helplessness she flung out her hands--"but we can't have a Hull House in every little town, you know, and I'm afraid we shouldn't find very many Jane Addamses if we did! Good girls don't need this sort of thing, and bad girls--well, unfortunately, the world has always had bad girls and always will have! We would merely turn our lovely clubhouse over to a lot of little romping hoydens."

"But--" began Mrs. Burgoyne eagerly.

"Just ONE moment," said the President, sweetly, and Mrs. Burgoyne sat down with blazing cheeks. "I only want to say that I think this is outside the purpose for which the club was formed," added Mrs. White. "If the club would care to vote on this, it seems to me that would be the wisest way of settling the matter; but perhaps we could hear from a few more members first?"

There was a little rustle of applause at this, and Sidney felt her heart give a sick plunge, and raged within herself because her own act had placed her at so great a disadvantage. In another moment, however, general attention was directed to a tall, plainly dressed, gentle woman, who rose and said rather shyly:

"Since you suggested our discussing this a little, Mrs. President, I would like to say that I like this idea very much myself. I've often felt that we weren't doing very much good, just uplifting ourselves, as it were, and I hope Mrs. Burgoyne will let me help her in any way I can, whether the club votes for or against this plan. I--I have four girls and boys of my own at home, as you know, and I find that even with plenty of music, and all the library books and company they want, it's hard enough to keep those children happy at night. And, ladies, there must be plenty of mothers over there in Old Paloma who worry about it as we do, and yet have no way of helping themselves. It seems to me we couldn't put our clubhouse to better use, or our time either, for that matter. I would vote decidedly 'yes' to such a plan. I've often felt that we--well, that we rather wasted some of our time here," she ended mildly.

"Thank you, Mrs. Moore," said Mrs. White politely.

"I hope it is part of your idea to let our own children have a part in the entertainments you propose," briskly added another woman, a clergyman's wife, rising immediately. "I think Doctor Babcock would thoroughly approve of the plan, and I am sure I do. Every little while," she went on smilingly, "my husband asks me what GOOD the club is doing, and I never can answer--"

"Men's clubs do so much good!" said some loud, cheerful voice at the back of the hall, and there was laughter.

"A great many of them do good and have side issues, like this one, that are all for good," the clergyman's wife responded quickly, "and personally I would thank God to be able to save even ten--to save even one--of those Old Paloma girls from a life of shame and suffering. I wish we had begun before. Mrs. Burgoyne may propose to build them their own clubhouse entirely herself; but if not, I hope we can all help in that too, when the time comes."

"Thank you, Mrs. Babcock," said the President coldly. "What do you think, Miss Pratt?"

"Oh, Mrs. Carew, and Mrs. Brown, and I all feel as Mrs. Burgoyne does," admitted Anne Pratt innocently, a little fluttered.

It was Mrs. White's turn to color.

"I didn't know that the matter had been discussed," she said stiffly.

"Only generally; not in reference to the club," Mrs. Burgoyne supplied quickly.

"I myself will propose an affirmative vote," said Mrs. Apostleman's rich old voice. Mrs. Apostleman was entirely indifferent to parliamentary law, and was never in order. "How d'ye do it? The ayes rise, is that it?"

She pulled herself magnificently erect by the chair-back in front of her, and with clapping and laughter the entire club rose to its feet.

"This is entirely out of order," said Mrs. White, very rosy. Everyone sat down suddenly, and the chairman gave two emphatic raps of her gavel.

The President then asked permission to speak, and moved, with great dignity, that the matter be laid before the board of directors at the next meeting, and, if approved, submitted in due order to the vote of the club.

The motion was briskly seconded, and a few minutes later Sidney found herself freed from the babel of voices and walking home with nervous rapidity. "Well, that's over!" she said once or twice aloud. "Thank Heaven, it's over!"

"Is your head better, Mother?" said Joanna, who had been hanging on the Hall gate waiting for her mother, and who put an affectionate arm about her as they walked up the path. "You LOOK better."

"Jo," said Mrs. Burgoyne seriously, "there's one sure cure for the blues in this world. I recommend it to you, for it's safer than cocaine, and just as sure. Go and do something you don't want to--for somebody else."

CHAPTER XVI

It was no pleasant prospect of a reunion at the club, or an evening with his old friends, that had taken Barry Valentine so suddenly to San Francisco, but a letter from his wife--or, rather, from his wife's mother, for Hetty herself never wrote--which had stirred a vague distrust and discomfort in his mind. Mrs. Scott, his mother-in-law, was a worldly, shrewd little person, but good-hearted, and as easily moved or stirred as a child. This was one of her characteristic letters, disconnected, ill-spelled, and scrawled upon scented lavender paper. She wrote that she and Hetty were sick of San Francisco, and they wanted Barry's permission to sell the Mission Street flats that afforded them a living, and go away once and for all. Het, her mother wrote, had had a fine offer for the houses; Barry's signature only was needed to close the deal.

All this might be true; it sounded reasonable enough; but, somehow, Barry fancied that it was not true, or at least that it was only partly so. What did Hetty want the money for, he wondered. Why should her mother reiterate so many times that if Barry for any possible reason disapproved, he was not to give the matter another thought; they most especially wanted only his simple yes or no. Why this consideration? Hetty had always been persistent enough about the things she wanted before. "I know you would consent if you could see how our hearts are set on this," wrote Mrs. Scott, "but if you say 'no,' that ends it."

"Sure, I'll sell," Barry said, putting the letter in his pocket. But it came persistently between him and his work. What mischief was Hetty in, he wondered. Had some get-rich-quick shark got hold of her; it was extremely likely. He could not shake the thought of her from his mind, her voice, her pretty, sullen little face, rose again and haunted him. What a child she had been, and what a boy he was, and how mistaken the whole bitter experience!

Walking home late at night, the memory of old days rode him like a hateful nightmare. He saw the little untidy flat they had had in New York; the white winter outside, and a deeper chill within; little Billy coughing and restless; Hetty practising her scales, and he, Barry, trying to write at one end of the dining-room table. He remembered how disappointment and restless ambition had blotted out her fresh, babyish beauty; how thin and sharp her voice had grown as the months went on.

Barry tried to read, but the book became mere printed words. He went softly into Billy's room, and sat down by the tumbled bed and the small warm sleeper. Billy, even asleep, snuggled his hand appreciatively into his father's, and brought its little fellow to lie there too, and pushed his head up against Barry's arm.

And there the father sat motionless, while the clock outside in the hall struck two, and three, and four. This was Hetty's baby, and where was Hetty? Alone with her little fretful mother, moving from boarding-house to boarding-house. Pretty no longer, buoyed up by the hope of an operatic career no longer, pinched--as they must be pinched--in money matters.

The thought came to him suddenly that he must see her; and though he fought it as unwelcome and distasteful, it grew rapidly into a conviction. He must see her again, must have a long talk with her, must ascertain that nothing he could do for the woman who had been his wife was left undone. He was no longer the exacting, unsuccessful boy she had left so unceremoniously; he was a man now, standing on his own feet, and with a recognized position in the community. The little fretful baby was a well-brushed young person who attended kindergarten and Sunday School. A new era of respectability and prosperity had set in. Hetty, his newly awakened sense of justice and his newly aroused ambition told him, must somehow share it. Not that there could ever be a complete reconciliation between them, but there could be good-will, there could be a readjustment and a friendlier understanding.

The thought of Sidney came suddenly upon his idle musings with a shock that made his heart sick. Gracious, beautiful, and fresh, although she was older than Hetty, how far she was removed from this sordid story of his, this darker side of his life! Perhaps months from now, his troubled thoughts ran on, he would tell her of his visit to Hetty. For he had determined to visit her.

Just at dawn he left the house and went out of his own gate. His face was pale, his eyes deeply ringed and his head ached furiously, but it was with a sort of content that he took his seat in the early train for San Francisco. He sank into a reverie, head propped on hand, that lasted until his journey was almost over; but once in the city, his old dread of seeing his wife came over him again, and it was only after a leisurely luncheon at the club that Barry took a Turk Street car to the dingy region where Hetty lived.

The row of dirty bay-windowed houses on either side of the street, and the dust and papers blowing about in the hot afternoon wind, somehow reminded him forcibly of old days and ways. With a sinking heart he went up one of the flights of wooden steps and asked at the door for Mrs. Valentine. A Japanese boy in his shirt-sleeves ushered him into a front room. This was evidently the "parlor"; hot sunlight streamed through the bay windows; there was an upright piano against the closed folding doors, and a graphophone on a dusty cherry table; wind whined at the window-casing; one or two big flies buzzed against the glass.

After a while Mrs. Smiley, the widow who conducted this little boarding-house, who was a cousin of Hetty and whom Barry had known years ago, came in. She was a tall, angular blonde, cheerlessly resigned to a cheerless existence. With her came a keen-faced, freckled boy of fourteen or fifteen, with his finger still marking a place in the book he had been reading aloud.

Hetty and her mother were out, it appeared. Mrs. Smiley didn't think they would be back to dinner; in fact, she reiterated nervously, she was sure they wouldn't. She was extremely and maddeningly non-committal. No, she didn't know why they wanted to sell the Mission Street flats. She had warned them it was a silly thing to bother Barry about it. No, she didn't know when he could see them tomorrow; she guessed, almost any time.

Barry went away full of uneasy suspicions, and more than ever convinced that something was wrong. He went back again the next morning, but nobody but the Japanese boy appeared to be at home. But a visit in the late afternoon was more successful, for he found Mrs. Smiley and the tall son again.

"Hetty IS here, isn't she?" he burst out suddenly, in the middle of a meaningless conversation. Mrs. Smiley turned pale and tried to laugh.

"Where else would she be?" she demanded, and she went back to her interrupted dissertation upon the unpleasantness of several specified boarders then under her roof.

"It is funny," Barry mused. "What did she say when she went out?"

"Why--" Mrs. Smiley began uncomfortably, "But, my gracious, I wish you would ask Aunt Ide, Barry!" she interrupted herself uncomfortably. "She'll tell you. She's the one to ask." Aunt Ide was Mrs. Scott.

"Tell me WHAT?" he persisted. "You tell me, Lulu; that's a dear."

"Auntie 'll tell you," she repeated, adding suddenly, to the boy, "Russy, wasn't Aunt Ide in her room when you went up? You run up and see."

"Nome," said Russell positively; but nevertheless he went.

"Nice kid, Lulu," said Barry in his idle way, "but he looks thin."

"He's the finest little feller God ever sent a woman," the mother answered with sudden passionate pride. Color leaped to her sallow cheeks. "But this house is no place for him to be cooped up reading all day," she went on in a worried tone, after a moment, "and I can't let him run with the boys around here; it's a regular gang. I don't know what I AM going to do with him. 'Tisn't as if he had a father."

"He wouldn't like to come up to me, and get broken on the Mail?" Barry queried in his interested way. "He'd get lots of fresh air, and he could sleep at my house. I'll keep an eye on him, if you say so."

"Go on the newspaper! I think he'd go crazy with joy," his mother said. Tears came into her faded eyes. "Barry, you're real good-hearted to offer it," she said gratefully. "Of all things in the world, that's the one Russ wants to do. But won't he be in your way?"

"He'll fit right in," Barry said. "Pack him up and send him along. If he doesn't like it, I guess his mother'll let him come home."

"Like it!" she echoed. Then in a lower tone she added, "You don't know what a load you're taking off my mind, Barry." She paused, colored again, and, to his surprise, continued rapidly, with a quick glance at the door, "Barry, I never did a thing like this before in my life, and I can't do it now. You know how much I owe Aunt Ide: she took me in, and did for me just as she did for Het, when I was a baby; she made my wedding dress, and she came right to me when Gus died, but I can't let you go back to Santa Paloma not knowing."

"Not knowing what?" Barry said, close upon the mystery at last.

"You know what Aunt Ide is," Mrs. Smiley said pleadingly. "There's not a mite of harm in her, but she just--You know she'd been signing Hetty's checks for a long time, Barry--"

"Go on," Barry said, as she paused distressedly.

"And she just went on--" Mrs. Smiley continued simply.

"Went on WHAT?" Barry demanded.

"After Het--went. Barry," the woman interrupted herself, "I oughtn't be the one to tell you, but don't you see--Don't you see Het's--"

"Dead," Barry heard his own voice say heavily. The cheap little room seemed to be closing in about him, he gripped the back of the chair by which he was standing. Mrs. Smiley began to cry quietly. They stood so for a long time.

After a while he sat down, and she told him about it, with that faithfulness to inessential detail that marks her class. Barry listened like a man in a dream. Mrs. Smiley begged him to stay to dinner to see "Aunt Ide," but he refused, and in the gritty dusk he found himself walking down the street, alone in silence at last. He took a car to the ocean beach, and far into the night sat on the rocks watching the dark play of the rolling Pacific, and listening to the steady rush and fall of the water.

The next day he saw his wife's mother, and at the sight of her frightened, fat little face, and the sound of the high voice he knew so well, the last shred of his anger and disgust vanished, and he could only pity her. He remembered how welcome she had made him to the little cottage in Plumas, those long years ago; how she had laughed at his youthful appreciation of her Sunday fried chicken and cherry pie, and the honest tears she had shed when he went, with the dimpled Hetty beside him, to tell her her daughter was won. She was Billy's grandmother, after all, and she had at least seen that Hetty was protected all through her misguided little career from the breath of scandal, and that Hetty's last days were made comfortable and serene.

He assured her gruffly that it was "all right," and she presently brightened, and told him through tears that he was a "king," when it was finally arranged that she should go on drawing the rents of the Mission Street property for the rest of her life. She and Mrs. Smiley persuaded him to dine with them, and he thought it quite characteristic of "Aunt Ide" to make a little occasion of it, and take them to a certain favored little French restaurant for the meal. But Mrs. Smiley was tremulous with gratitude and relief, Russell's face was radiant, his adoring eyes all for Barry, and Barry, always willing to accept a situation gracefully, really enjoyed his dinner.

He stayed in San Francisco another day and went to Hetty's grave, high up in the Piedmont Hills, and took a long lonely tramp above the college town afterward. Early the next morning he started for home, fresh from a bath and a good breakfast, and feeling now, for the first time, that he was free, and that it was good to be free--free to work and to plan his life, and free, his innermost consciousness exulted to realize, to go to her some day, the Lady of his Heart's Desire, and take her, with all the fragrance and beauty that were part of her, into his arms. And oh, the happy years ahead; he seemed to feel the sweetness of spring winds blowing across them, and the glow of winter fires making them bright! What of her fabulous wealth, after all, if he could support her as she chose to live, a simple country gentle-woman, in a little country town?

Barry stared out at the morning fields and hills, where fog and sunshine were holding their daily battle, and his heart sang within him.

Fog held the field at Santa Paloma when he reached it, the station building dripped somberly. Main Street was but a line of vague shapes in the mist. No grown person was in sight, but Barry was not ten feet from the train before a screaming horde of small boys was upon him, with shouted news in which he recognized the one word, over and over:

"Fire!"

It took him a few minutes to get the sense of what they said. He stared at them dully. But when he first repeated it to himself aloud, it seemed already old news; he felt as if he had known it for a very long time: "The MAIL office caught fire yesterday, and the whole thing is burned to the ground."

"Caught fire yesterday, and the whole thing is burned to the ground: yes, of course," Barry said. He was not conscious of starting for the scene, he was simply there. A fringe of idle watchers, obscured in the fog, stood about the sunken ruins of what had been the MAIL building. Barry joined them.

He did not answer when a dozen sympathetic murmurs addressed him, because he was not conscious of hearing a single voice. He stood silently, looking down at the twisted great knots of metal that had been the new presses, the great wave of soaked and half-burned newspapers that had been the last issue of the MAIL. The fire had been twenty-four hours ago, but the ruins were still smoking. Lengths of charred woodwork, giving forth a sickening odor, dripped water still; here and there brave little spurts of flame still sucked noisily. A twisted typewriter stood erect in steaming ashes; a lunch-basket, with a red, fringed napkin in it, had somehow escaped with only a wetting. Barry noticed that the walls of the German bakery next door were badly singed, that one show-window was cracked across, and that the frosted wedding-cake inside stood in a pool of dirty water.

He was presently aware that someone was telling him that nobody was to blame. Details were volunteered, and he listened quietly, like a dispassionate onlooker. "Hits you pretty hard, Barry," sympathetic voices said.

"Ruins me," he answered briefly.

And it dawned upon him sickly and certainly that it was true. He was ruined now. All his hopes had been rooted here, in what was now this mass of wet ashes steaming up into the fog. Here had been his chance for a livelihood, and a name; his chance to stand before the community for what was good, and strong, and helpful. He had been proud because his editorials were beginning to be quoted here and there; he had been keenly ambitious for Sidney's plans, her hopes for Old Paloma. How vain it all was now, and how preposterous it seemed that only an hour ago he had let his thoughts of the future include her--always so far above him, and now so infinitely removed!

She would be sympathetic, he knew; she would be all kindness and generosity. And perhaps, six months ago, he would have accepted more generosity from her; but Barry had found himself now, and he knew that she had done for him all he would let her do.

He smiled suddenly and grimly as he remembered another bridge, just burned behind him. If he had not promised Hetty's mother that her income should go on uninterruptedly, he might have pulled something out of this wreckage, after all. For a moment he speculated: he COULD sell the Mission Street property now; he might even revive the MAIL, after a while--

But no, what was promised was promised, after all, and poor little Mrs. Scott must be left to what peace and pleasure the certainty of an income gave her. And he must begin again, somehow, somewhere, burdened with a debt, burdened with a heartache, burdened with--His heart turned with sudden warmth to the thought of Billy; Billy at least, staunch little partner of so many dark days, and bright, should not be counted a burden.

Even as he thought of his son, a small warm hand slid into his with a reassuring pressure, and lie looked down to see the little figure beside him. Moment after moment went by, timid shafts of gold sunshine were beginning to conquer the mist now, and still father and son stood silent, hand in hand.

CHAPTER XVII

The mischief was done; no use to stand there by the smoking ruins of what had been his one real hope for himself and his life. After a while Barry roused himself. There seemed to be nothing to do at the moment, no more to be said. He and Billy walked up River Street to their own gate, but when they reached it, Barry, obeying an irresistible impulse, merely left his coat and suit-case there, and went on through the Hall gateway, and up to the house.

The sun was coming out bravely now, and already he felt its warmth in the garden. Everywhere the fog was rising, was fading against the green of the trees. He followed a delicious odor of wood smoke and the sound of voices, to the barnyard, and here found the lady of the house, with her inevitable accompaniment of interested children. Sidney was managing an immense brush fire with a long pole; her gingham skirt pinned back trimly over a striped petticoat, her cheeks flushed, her hair riotous under a gipsy hat.

At Barry's first word she dropped her pole, her whole face grew radiant, and she came toward him holding out both her hands.

"Barry!" she said eagerly, her eyes trying to read his face, "how glad I am you've come! We didn't know how to reach you. You've heard, of course--! You've seen--?"

"The poor old MAIL? Yes, I'm just from there," he said soberly. "Can we talk?"

"As long as you like," she answered briskly. And after some directions to the children, she led him to the little garden seat below the side porch, and they sat down. "Barry, you look tired," she said then. "Do you know, I don't know where you've been all these days, or what you went for? Was it to San Francisco?"

"San Francisco, yes," he assented, "I didn't dream I'd be there so long." He rubbed his forehead with a weary hand. "I'll tell you all about it presently," he said. "I had a letter from my wife's mother that worried me, and I started off at half-cock, I got worrying--but of course I should have written you--"

"Don't bother about that now, if it distresses you," she said quickly and sympathetically. "Any time will do for that. I--I knew it was something serious," she went on, relief in her voice, "or you wouldn't have simply disappeared that way! I--I said so. Barry, are you hungry?"

He tried to laugh at the maternal attitude that was never long absent in her, but the tears came into his eyes instead. After all the strain and sleeplessness and despondency, it was too poignantly sweet to find her so simply cheering and trustful, in her gipsy dress, with the brightening sunlight and the sweet old garden about her. Barry could have dropped on his knees to bury his face in her skirts, and feel the motherly hands on his hair, but instead he admitted honestly to hunger and fatigue.

Sidney vanished at once, and presently came back followed by her black cook, both carrying a breakfast that Barry was to enjoy at once under the rose vines. Sidney poured his coffee, and sat contentedly nibbling toast while he fell upon the cold chicken and blackberries.

"Now," said her heartening voice, "we'll talk! What is to be done first about the MAIL?"

"No insurance, you know," he began at once. "We never did carry any in the old days and I suppose that's why I didn't. So that makes it a dead loss. Worse than that--for I wasn't clear yet, you know. The safe they carried out; so the books are all right, I suppose, although they say we had better not open it for a few days. Then I can settle everything up as far as possible. And after that--well, I've been thinking that perhaps Barker, of the San Francisco TELEGRAM might give me a start of some sort--" He rumpled his hair with a desperate gesture. "The thing's come on me like such a thunderbolt that I really haven't thought it out!" he ended apologetically.

"The thing's come on you like such a thunderbolt," she echoed cheerfully, "that you aren't taking it like yourself at all! The question, is if we work like Trojans from now on, can we get an issue of the MAIL out tomorrow?"

"Get an issue out tomorrow!" he repeated, staring at her.

"Certainly. I would have done what I could about it," said Sidney briskly, "but not knowing where you were, or when you were coming back, my hands were absolutely tied. Now, Barry, LISTEN!" she broke off, not reassured by his expression, "and don't jump at the conclusion that it's impossible. What would it mean?"

"To get an issue of the MAIL out tomorrow? Why, great Scott, Sid, you don't seem to realize that there's not a stick left standing!"

"I do realize. I was there until the fire was out," she said calmly.
And for a few minutes they talked of the fire. Then she said abruptly:
"Would Ferguson let you use the old STAR PRESS for a few weeks, do you
think?"

"I don't see why he should," Barry said perversely.

"I don't see why he shouldn't. I'll tell you something you don't know.
Night before last, Barry, while I was down in the office, old Ferguson
himself came in, and poked about, and asked various questions. Finally
he asked me what I thought the chances were of your wanting to buy out
the Star. What do you think at THAT?"

"He's sick of it, is he?" Barry said, with kindling eyes. "Well, we've
seen that coming, haven't we? I will be darned!" He shook his head
regretfully. "That would have been a big thing for the MAIL" he said,
"but it's all up now!"

"Not necessarily," the lady undauntedly rejoined. "I've been thinking,
Barry," she went on, "if you reordered the presses, they'd give you
plenty of time to pay for them, wouldn't they? Might even take
something off the price, under the circumstances?"

"I suppose they might." He made an impatient gesture. "But that's just
one--"

"One item, I know. But it's the main item. Then you could rent the
office and loft over the old station, couldn't you? And move the old
Star press in there this afternoon."

"This afternoon," said Barry calmly.

"Well, we don't gain anything by waiting. You can write a manly and affecting editorial,"--her always irrepressible laughter broke out, "full of allusions to the phoenix, you know! And my regular Saturday column is all done, and Miss Porter can send in something, and there's any amount of stuff about the Folsom lawsuit. And Young, Mason and Company ought to take at least a page to advertise their premium day to-morrow. I'll come down as soon as you've moved--"

Barry reached for his hat.

"The thing can't be done," he announced firmly, "but, by George, Sid, you would give a field mouse courage! And what a grandstand play, if we COULD put it through! There's not a second to be lost, though. But look here," and with sudden gravity he took both her hands, "it'll take some more money, you know."

"I have some more money," she answered serenely.

"Well, I'll GET some!" he declared emphatically. "It won't be so much, either, once we get started. And so old Ferguson wanted to sell, did he?"

"He did. And we'll buy the STAR yet." They were on the path now. "Telephone me when you can," she said, "and don't lose a minute now! Good luck!"

And Barry's great stride had taken him half-way down River Street, his hands in his pockets, his mind awhirl with plans, before it occurred to him that he had not told her the news of Hetty, after all.

CHAPTER XVIII

On that same afternoon, several of the most influential members of the Santa Paloma Woman's Club met informally at Mrs. Carew's house. Some of the directors were there, Miss Pratt, Mrs. Lloyd and Mrs. Adams, and of course Mrs. White, who had indeed been instrumental in arranging the meeting. They had met to discuss Mrs. Burgoyne's plan of using the clubhouse as a meeting place for the Old Paloma factory girls. All these ladies were quite aware that their verdict, however unofficial, would influence the rest of the club, and that what this group of a dozen or fifteen decided upon to-day would practically settle the matter.

Mrs. Willard White, hitherto serenely supreme in this little world, was curiously upset about the whole thing, openly opposed to Mrs. Burgoyne's suggestion, and surprised that her mere wish in the matter was not sufficient to carry a negative vote. Her contention was that the clubhouse had been built for very different purposes than those Mrs. Burgoyne proposed, and that charity to the Old Paloma girls had no part in the club's original reasons for being. She meant, in the course of the argument, to hint that while so many of the actual necessities of decent living were lacking in the factory settlement homes, mere dancing and moving-pictures did not appeal to her as reasonable or right; and although uneasily aware that she supported the unpopular argument, still she was confident of an eventual triumph.

But despite the usual laughter, and the pleasantries and compliments, there was an air of deadly earnestness about the gathered club-women today that bespoke a deeper interest than was common in the matter up for discussion. The President's color rose and deepened steadily, as the afternoon wore on, and one voice after another declared for the new plan, and her arguments became a little less impersonal and a little more sharp. This was especially noticeable when, as was inevitable, the name of Mrs. Burgoyne was introduced.

"I personally feel," said Mrs. White finally, "that perhaps we Santa Paloma women are just a little bit undignified when we allow a perfect stranger to come in among us, and influence our lives so materially, JUST because she happens to be a multi-millionaire. Are we so swayed by mere money? I hope not. I hope we all live our lives as suits US best, not to please--or shall I say flatter, and perhaps win favor with?--a rich woman. We--some of us, that is!"--her smile was all lenience--"have suddenly decided we can dress more simply, have suddenly decided to put our girls into gingham rompers, and instead of giving them little dancing parties, let them play about like boys! We wonder why we need spend our money on imported hats and nice dinners and hand-embroidered underwear, and Oriental rugs, although we thought these things very well worth having a few months ago--and why? Just because we are easily led, I'm afraid, and not quite conscious enough of our own dignity!"

There had been a decided heightening of color among the listening women during this little speech, and, as the President finished, more than one pair of eyes rested upon her with a slightly resentful steadiness. There was a short silence, in which several women were gathering their thoughts for speech, but Mrs. Brown, always popular in Santa Paloma, from the days of her short braids and short dresses, and quite the youngest among them to-day, was the first to speak.

"I daresay that is quite true, Mrs. White," said Mrs. Brown, with dignity, "except that I don't think Mrs. Burgoyne's money influences me, or any of us! I admit that she herself, quite apart from her great fortune, has influenced me tremendously in lots of ways, but I don't think she ever tried to do it, or realizes that she has. And as far as copying goes, don't we women always copy somebody, anyway? Aren't we always imitating the San Francisco women, and don't they copy New York, and doesn't New York copy London or Paris? We read what feathers are in, and how skirts are cut, and how coffee and salads are served, and we all do it, or try to. And when Mrs. Burgoyne came to the Hall, and never took one particle of interest in that sort of thing, I just thought it over and wondered why I should attempt to impress a woman who could buy this whole town and not miss the money?"

Laughter interrupted her, and some sympathetic clapping, but she presently went on seriously:

"I took all the boys' white socks one day, and dyed them dark brown. And I dyed all their white suits dark blue. I've gotten myself some galatea dresses that nothing tears or spoils, and that come home fresh and sweet from the wash every week. And, as a result, I actually have some time to spare, for the first time since I was married. We are going to try some educational experiments on the children this winter, and, if that leaves any leisure, I am heart and soul for this new plan. Doctor Brown feels as I do. Of course, he's a doctor," said the loyal little wife, "and he KNOWS! And he says that all those Old Paloma girls want is a little mothering, and that when there are mothers enough to go round, there won't be any charity or legislation needed in this world."

"I think you've said it all, for all of us, Mary!" Mrs. Carew said, when some affectionate applause had subsided. "I think things were probably different, a few generations ago," she went on, "but nowadays when fashions are so arbitrary, and change so fast, really and honestly, some of us, whose incomes are limited, will have to stop somewhere. Why, the very children expect box-parties, and motor-trips, and caterers' suppers, in these days. And one wouldn't mind, if it left time for home life, and reading, and family intercourse, but it doesn't. We don't know what our children are studying, what they're thinking about, or what life means to them at all, because we are too busy answering the telephone, and planning clothes, and writing formal notes, and going to places we feel we ought to be seen in. I'm having more fun than I had in years, helping our children plan some abridged plays from Shakespeare, with the Burgoyne girls, for this winter, and I'm perfectly astonished, even though I'm their mother, at their enjoyment of it, and at my own. Mr. Carew himself, who NEVER takes much interest in that sort of thing, asked me why they couldn't give them for the Old Paloma Girls' Club, if they get a club room. I didn't know he even knew anything about our club plans. I said, 'George, are you willing to have Jeannette get interested in that crowd?' and he said, 'Finest thing in the world for her!' and I don't know," finished Mrs. Carew, thoughtfully, "but what he's right."

"I'm all for it," said breezy Mrs. Lloyd, "I don't imagine I'd be any good at actually talking to them, but I would go to the dances, and introduce people, and trot partners up to the wallflowers--"

There was more laughter, and then Mrs. Adams said briskly:

"Well, let's take an informal vote!"

"I don't think that's necessary, Sue," said Mrs. White, generously, "I think I am the only one of us who believes in preserving the tradition of the dear old club, and I must bow to the majority, of course. Perhaps it will be a little hard to see strangers there; our pretty floors ruined, and our pretty walls spotted, but--" an eloquent shrug, and a gesture of her pretty hands finished the sentence with the words, "isn't that the law?"

And upon whole-hearted applause for Mrs. White, Mrs. Carew tactfully introduced the subject of tea.

They were all chatting amicably enough in the dining-room a few minutes
later when George Carew and Barry Valentine came in. Barry, who seemed
excited, exhilarated and tired, had come to borrow a typewriter from
the Carews. He responded to sympathetic inquiries, that he had been
working like a madman since noon, and that there would be an issue of
the Mail ready for them in the morning. He said, "everyone had been
simply corking about everything," and it began to look like smooth
sailing now. In the few minutes that he waited for young George Carew
to find the typewriter and bring it down to him, a fresh interruption
occurred in the entrance of old Mrs. Apostleman.

Mrs. Apostleman, between being out of breath from hurrying up the hill
in the late afternoon heat, and fearful that the gathering would break
up before she could say what she wanted to say, and entirely unable to
control her gasping and puffing, was a sight at once funny and
pitiable. As she sank into a comfortable chair she held up one fat hand
to command attention, and with the other laid forcible hold upon Barry
Valentine. Three or four of the younger women hurried to her with fans
and tea, and in a moment or two she really could manage disconnected
words.

"Thanks, me dear. No, no cake. Just a mouthful of tea to--there, that's
better! I was afraid ye'd all be gone--that'll do, thank ye, Susie!
Well," she set down her tea-cup, "well! I've a little piece of news for
you all--don't go, Barry, you'll be interested in this, and I couldn't
wait to come up and tell ye!" She began to fumble in her bag, and
presently produced therefrom her eye-glasses and a letter. The latter
she opened with a great crackling of paper.

"This is from me brother, Alexander Wetherall," said she, with an
impressive glance over her glasses. "As ye know, he's a family lawyer
in New York, he has the histories of half the old families in the
country pigeon-holed away in those old offices of his. He doesn't write

me very often; his wife does now and then--stupid woman, but nice. However, I wrote him in May, and told him Mrs. Burgoyne had bought the Hall, and just asked him what he knew about her and her people. Here--" marking a certain line with a pudgy, imperative finger, she handed a page of the letter to Barry, "read from there on," she commanded, "this is what he says."

Barry took the paper, but hesitated.

"It's all right!" said the old lady, impatiently, "nobody could say anything that wasn't good about Sidney Burgoyne."

Thus reassured, Barry turned obediently to the indicated place.

"'You ask me about your new neighbor,'" he read, "'I suppose of course you know that she is Paul Frothingham's only child by his second marriage. Her mother died while she was a baby, and Frothingham took her all over the world with him, wherever he went. She married very young, Colonel John Burgoyne, of the Maryland family, older than she, but a very fine fellow. As a girl and as his wife she had an extraordinary opportunity for social success, she was a great favorite in the diplomatic circle at Washington, and well known in the best London set, and in the European capitals. She seems to be quite a remarkable young woman, but you are all wrong about her money; she is very far from rich. She--'"

Barry stopped short. Mrs. Apostleman cackled delightedly; no one else stirred.

"'She got very little of Frothingham's money,'" Barry presently read on, "'it came to him from his first wife, who was a widow with two daughters when he married her. The money naturally reverted to her girls, Mrs. Fred Senior and Mrs. Spencer Mack, both of this city.'"

"Ha! D'ye get that?" said Mrs. Apostleman. "Go on!"

"'Frothingham left his own daughter something considerably less than a hundred thousand dollars,'" Barry presently resumed, "'not more than seventy or eighty thousand, certainly. It is still invested in the estate. It must pay her three or four thousand a year. And besides that she has only Burgoyne's insurance, twenty or twenty-five thousand, for those years of illness pretty well used up his own money. I believe the stepsisters were very anxious to make her a more generous arrangement, but she seems to have declined it. Alice says they are quite devoted--'"

"Alice don't count!" said the old lady "that's his wife. That's enough." She stopped the reader and refolded the letter, her mischievous eyes dancing. "Well, what d'ye think of that?" she demanded.

Barry's bewildered, "Well, I will be darned!" set loose a babel of tongues. Mrs. Apostleman had not counted in vain upon a sensation; everyone talked at once. Mrs. White's high, merry laugh dominated all the other voices.

"So there is a very much better reason for this simple-dinner-blue-gingham existence than we supposed," said the President of the Santa Paloma Women's Club amusedly when the first rush of comment died away. "I think that is quite delicious! While all of us were feeling how superior she was not to get a motor, and not to rebuild the Hall, she was simply living within her income, and making the best of it!"

"I don't know that it makes her any less superior," Mrs. Carew said thoughtfully. "It--it certainly makes her seem--NICER. I never suspected her of--well, of preaching, exactly, but I have sometimes thought that she really couldn't enter into our point of view, with all that money! I think I'm going to like her more than ever!" she finished laughingly.

"Why, it's the greatest relief in the world!" exclaimed Mrs. Adams. "I've been rather holding back about going up there, and imitating her, because I honestly didn't want to be influenced by eight millions, and I was afraid. I WAS. Not a week ago Wayne asked me if I thought she'd like him to donate a sewing machine to her Girls' Club for them to run up their little costumes with--he has the agency, you know--and I said, 'Oh, don't, Wayne, she can buy them a sewing machine apiece if she wants to, and never know it!' But I'm going to make him write her, TO-NIGHT," said Mrs. Adams, firmly, "and I declare I feel as if a weight had dropped off my shoulders. It MEANS so much more now, if we offer her the club. It means that we aren't merely giving a Lady Bountiful her way, but that we're all working together like neighbors, and trying to do some good in the world."

"And I don't think there's any question that she would live exactly this way," Miss Pratt contributed shyly, "and play with the children, and dress as she does, even if she had fifty millions! She's simply found out what pays in this life, and what doesn't pay, and I think a good many of us were living too hard and fast ever to stop and think whether it was really worth while or not. She's the happiest woman I ever knew; it makes one happy just to be with her, and no money can buy that."

"But it's curious she never has taken the trouble to undeceive us," said Mrs. White beginning to fit on an immaculate pair of white gloves, finger by finger.

"Why--you'll see!--She never dreamed we thought she was anything but one of ourselves." Mrs. Brown predicted. "Why should she? When did she ever speak of money, or take the least interest in money? She never speaks of it. She says 'I can't afford the time, or I can't afford the effort,' that's what counts with her. Doesn't it, Barry?"

"Barry, do you really suppose--" Mrs. Carew was beginning, as she turned to the doorway where he had been standing.

But Barry had gone.

CHAPTER XIX

Barry went straight up to the Hall, but Sidney was not there. Joanna and Ellen, busily murmuring over "Flower Ladies" on the wide terrace steps, told him that Mother was to be late to supper, and, with obviously forced hospitality and one eye upon their little families of inverted roses and hollyhocks, asked him to wait. Barry thanked them, but couldn't wait.

He went like a man in a dream down River Street, past gardens that glowed with fragrant beauty, and under the great trees and the warm, sunset sky. And what a good world it seemed to be alive in, and what a friendly village in which to find work and love and content. A dozen returning householders, stopping at their gates, wanted the news of his venture, a dozen freshly-clad, interested women, watering lawns in the shade, called out to wish him good fortune. And always, before his eyes, the thought of the vanished millions danced like a star. She was not infinitely removed, she was not set apart by great fortune, she was only the sweetest and best of women, to be wooed and won like any other. He ran upstairs and flung open the door of the little bare new office of the MAIL, like an impetuous boy. There was no one there. But a wide white hat with a yellow rose pinned on it hung above the new oak

desk in the corner, and his heart rose at the sight. His own desk had
an improvised drop light hung over it; he lowered the typewriter from
his cramped arm upon a mass of clippings and notes. Beyond this room
was the great bare loft, where two or three oily men were still toiling
in the fading light over the establishing of the old STAR press. Sashes
had been taken from one of the big windows to admit the entrance of the
heavier parts; thick pulley ropes dangled at the sill. Great unopened
bundles of gray paper filled the center of the floor, a slim amused
youth was putting the finishing touches to a telephone on the wall, and
Sidney, bare-headed, very business-like and keenly interested, was
watching everybody and making suggestions. She greeted Barry with a
cheerful wave of the hand.

"There you are!" she said, relievedly. "Come and see what you think of
this. Do you know this office is going to be much nicer than the old
one? How goes everything with you?"

"Like lightning!" he answered. "At this rate, there's nothing to it at
all. Have the press boys showed up yet?"

"They are over at the hotel, getting their dinners," she explained.
"And we have borrowed lamps from the hotel to use here this evening.
Did you hear that Martin, of the Press, you know, has offered to send
over the A.P. news as fast as it comes in? Isn't that very decent of
him? Here's Miss Porter's stuff."

She sat down, and began to assort papers on her desk, quite absorbed in
what she was doing. Barry, at his own desk, opened and shut a drawer or
two noisily, but he was really watching her, with a thumping heart.
Watching the bare brown head, the lowered lashes, the mouth that moved
occasionally in time with her busy thoughts--

Suddenly she looked up, and their eyes met.

Without the faintest consciousness of what he did, Barry crossed the floor between them, and as, on an equally unconscious impulse, she stood up, paling and breathless, he laid his hand over hers on the littered desk, and they stood so, staring at each other, the desk between them.

"Sidney," he said incoherently, "who--where--where did your father's money go--who got it?"

She looked at him in utter bewilderment.

"Where did WHAT--father's money? Who got it? Are you crazy, Barry?" she stammered.

"Ah, Sidney, tell me! Did it come to you?"

"Why--why--" She seemed suddenly to understand that there was some reason for the question, and answered quite readily: "It belonged to my father's first wife, Barry, most of it. And it went to her daughters, my step-sisters, they are older than I and both married--"

"Then you're NOT worth eight million dollars?"

"I--? Why, you know I'm not!" Her eyes were at their widest. "Who ever said I was? _I_ never said so!"

"But everyone in town thinks so!" Barry's great sigh of relief came from his very soul.

Sidney, pale before, grew very red. She freed her hands, and sat down.

"Well, they are very silly, then!" she said, almost crossly. And as the thought expanded, she added, "But I don't see how anyone COULD! They must have thought my letting them help me out with the Flower Show and begging for the Old Paloma girls was a nice piece of affectation! If I had eight million dollars, or one million, don't you suppose I'd be DOING something, instead of puttering away with just the beginning of things!" The annoyed color deepened. "I hope you're mistaken, Barry," said she. "Why didn't you set them right?"

"I! Why, I thought so too!"

"Oh, Barry! What a hypocrite you must have thought me!" She buried her rosy face in her hand for a moment. Presently she rushed on, half indignantly, "--With all my talk about the sinfulness of American women, who persistently attempt a scheme of living that is far beyond their incomes! And talking of the needs of the poor all over the world, with all that money lying idle!"

"I thought of it chiefly as an absolute and immovable barrier between us," Barry said honestly, "and that was as far as my thinking went."

Her eyes met his with that curious courage she had when a difficult moment had to be faced.

"There is a more serious barrier than that between us," she reminded him gravely.

"Hetty!" he said stupidly. "But I TOLD you--"

But he stopped short, realizing that he had not yet told her, and rather at a loss.

"You didn't tell me anything," she said, eyeing him steadily.

"Why," Barry's tone was much lower, "I meant to tell you first of all, but--you know what a day I have had! It seems impossible that I only left San Francisco this morning."

He brought his chair from his own desk, and sat opposite her, and, while the summer twilight outside deepened into dusk, unmindful of time, he went over the pitiful little story. Sidney listened, her serious eyes never leaving his face, her fine hands locked idly before her. The telephone boy and the movers had gone now, and there was silence all about.

"You have suffered enough, Barry; thank God it is all over!" she said, at the end, "and we know," she went on, with one of her rare revelations of the spiritual deeps that lay so close to the surface of her life, "we know that she is safe and satisfied at last, in His care." For a moment her absent eyes seemed to fathom far spaces. Barry abruptly broke the silence.

"For one year, Sidney," he said, in a purposeful, steady voice that was new to her, and that brought her eyes, almost startled, to his face, "for one year I'm going to show you what I can do. In that time the Mail will be where it was before the fire, if all goes well. And then--"

"Then--" she said, a little unsteadily, rising and gathering hat and gloves together, "then you shall come to me and tell me anything you like! But--but not now! All this is so new and so strange--"

"Ah, but Sidney!" he pleaded, taking her hands again, "mayn't I speak of it just this one day, and then never again? Let me think for this whole year that PERHAPS you will marry a country editor, and that we shall spend the rest of our lives together, writing and planning, and tramping through the woods, and picnicking with the kiddies on the river, and giving Christmas parties for every little rag-tag and bob-tail in Old Paloma!"

"But you don't want to settle down in this stupid village," she laughed tremulously, tears on her lashes, "at the ugly old Hall, and among these superficial empty-headed women?"

"Just here," he said, smiling at his own words, "in the sweetest place in the world, among the best neighbors! I never want to go anywhere else. Our friends are here, our work is here--"

"And we are here!" she finished it for him, laughing. Barry, with a great rising breath, put his arms about the white figure, and crushed her to him, and Sidney laid her hand on his shoulder, and raised her face honestly for his first kiss.

"And now let me go home to my neglected girls," she said, after an interval. "You have a busy night ahead of you, and your press boys will be here any minute."

But first she took a sheet of yellow copy paper, and wrote on it, "One year of silence. August thirtieth to August thirtieth." "Is this inclusive?" she asked, looking up.

"Exclusive," said Barry, firmly.

"Exclusive," she echoed obediently. And when she had added the word, she folded the sheet and gave it to Barry. "There is a little reminder for you," said she.

Barry went down to the street door with her, to watch her start homeward in the sweet summer darkness.

"Oh, one more thing I meant to say," she said, as they stood on the platform of what had been the old station, "I don't know why I haven't said it already, or why you haven't."

"And that is, Madam--?" he asked attentively.

"It's just this," she swayed a little nearer to him--her laughing voice was no more than a whisper. "I love you, Barry!"

"Haven't I said that?" he asked a little hoarsely.

"Not yet."

"Then I say it," he answered steadily, "I love you, my darling!"

"Oh, not here, Barry--in the street!" was Mrs. Burgoyne's next remark.

But there was no moon, and no witnesses but the blank walls and shuttered windows of neighboring storehouses. And the silent year had not, after all, fairly begun.

The Codes Of Hammurabi And Moses
W. W. Davies

QTY

The discovery of the Hammurabi Code is one of the greatest achievements of archaeology, and is of paramount interest, not only to the student of the Bible, but also to all those interested in ancient history...

Religion   ISBN: *1-59462-338-4*   **Pages:132**
MSRP $12.95

The Theory of Moral Sentiments
Adam Smith

QTY

This work from 1749. contains original theories of conscience amd moral judgment and it is the foundation for systemof morals.

Philosophy   ISBN: *1-59462-777-0*   **Pages:536**
MSRP $19.95

Jessica's First Prayer
Hesba Stretton

QTY

In a screened and secluded corner of one of the many railway-bridges which span the streets of London there could be seen a few years ago, from five o'clock every morning until half past eight, a tidily set-out coffee-stall, consisting of a trestle and board, upon which stood two large tin cans, with a small fire of charcoal burning under each so as to keep the coffee boiling during the early hours of the morning when the work-people were thronging into the city on their way to their daily toil...

Childrens   ISBN: *1-59462-373-2*   **Pages:84**
MSRP $9.95

My Life and Work
Henry Ford

QTY

Henry Ford revolutionized the world with his implementation of mass production for the Model T automobile. Gain valuable business insight into his life and work with his own auto-biography... "We have only started on our development of our country we have not as yet, with all our talk of wonderful progress, done more than scratch the surface. The progress has been wonderful enough but..."

Biographies/   ISBN: *1-59462-198-5*   **Pages:300**
MSRP $21.95

The Art of Cross-Examination
Francis Wellman

QTY

I presume it is the experience of every author, after his first book is published upon an important subject, to be almost overwhelmed with a wealth of ideas and illustrations which could readily have been included in his book, and which to his own mind, at least, seem to make a second edition inevitable. Such certainly was the case with me; and when the first edition had reached its sixth impression in five months, I rejoiced to learn that it seemed to my publishers that the book had met with a sufficiently favorable reception to justify a second and considerably enlarged edition. ..

Pages:412

Reference   ISBN: *1-59462-647-2*   *MSRP $19.95*

On the Duty of Civil Disobedience
Henry David Thoreau

QTY

Thoreau wrote his famous essay, On the Duty of Civil Disobedience, as a protest against an unjust but popular war and the immoral but popular institution of slave-owning. He did more than write—he declined to pay his taxes,   and was hauled off to gaol in consequence. Who can say how much this refusal of his hastened the end of the war and of slavery ?

Law   ISBN: *1-59462-747-9*   **Pages:48**   *MSRP $7.45*

Dream Psychology Psychoanalysis for Beginners
Sigmund Freud

QTY

Sigmund Freud, born Sigismund Schlomo Freud (May 6, 1856 - September 23, 1939), was a Jewish-Austrian neurologist and psychiatrist who co-founded the psychoanalytic school of psychology. Freud is best known for his theories of the unconscious mind, especially involving the mechanism of repression; his redefinition of sexual desire as mobile and directed towards a wide variety of objects; and his therapeutic techniques, especially his understanding of transference in the therapeutic relationship and the presumed value of dreams as sources of insight into unconscious desires.

Pages:196

Dream Psychology
Psychoanalysis for Beginners

Sigmund Freud

Psychology   ISBN: *1-59462-905-6*   *MSRP $15.45*

The Miracle of Right Thought
Orison Swett Marden

QTY

Believe with all of your heart that you will do what you were made to do. When the mind has once formed the habit of holding cheerful, happy, prosperous pictures, it will not be easy to form the opposite habit. It does not matter how improbable or how far away this realization may see, or how dark the prospects may be, if we visualize them as best we can, as vividly as possible, hold tenaciously to them and vigorously struggle to attain them, they will gradually become actualized, realized in the life. But a desire, a longing without endeavor, a yearning abandoned or held indifferently will vanish without realization.

Pages:360

Self Help   ISBN: *1-59462-644-8*   *MSRP $25.45*

www.bookjungle.com *email: sales@bookjungle.com fax: 630-214-0564 mail: Book Jungle PO Box 2226 Champaign, IL 61825*

QTY

The Rosicrucian Cosmo-Conception Mystic Christianity *by Max Heindel* ISBN: *1-59462-188-8* **$38.95**
The Rosicrucian Cosmo-conception is not dogmatic, neither does it appeal to any other authority than the reason of the student. It is: not controversial, but is: sent forth in the, hope that it may help to clear... New Age/Religion Pages 646

Abandonment To Divine Providence *by Jean-Pierre de Caussade* ISBN: *1-59462-228-0* **$25.95**
"The Rev. Jean Pierre de Caussade was one of the most remarkable spiritual writers of the Society of Jesus in France in the 18th Century. His death took place at Toulouse in 1751. His works have gone through many editions and have been republished... Inspirational/Religion Pages 400

Mental Chemistry *by Charles Haanel* ISBN: *1-59462-192-6* **$23.95**
Mental Chemistry allows the change of material conditions by combining and appropriately utilizing the power of the mind. Much like applied chemistry creates something new and unique out of careful combinations of chemicals the mastery of mental chemistry... New Age Pages 354

The Letters of Robert Browning and Elizabeth Barret Barrett 1845-1846 vol II ISBN: *1-59462-193-4* **$35.95**
by Robert Browning and Elizabeth Barrett Biographies Pages 596

Gleanings In Genesis (volume I) *by Arthur W. Pink* ISBN: *1-59462-130-6* **$27.45**
Appropriately has Genesis been termed "the seed plot of the Bible" for in it we have, in germ form, almost all of the great doctrines which are afterwards fully developed in the books of Scripture which follow... Religion/Inspirational Pages 420

The Master Key *by L. W. de Laurence* ISBN: *1-59462-001-6* **$30.95**
In no branch of human knowledge has there been a more lively increase of the spirit of research during the past few years than in the study of Psychology, Concentration and Mental Discipline. The requests for authentic lessons in Thought Control, Mental Discipline and... New Age/Business Pages 422

The Lesser Key Of Solomon Goetia *by L. W. de Laurence* ISBN: *1-59462-092-X* **$9.95**
This translation of the first book of the "Lernegton" which is now for the first time made accessible to students of Talismanic Magic was done, after careful collation and edition, from numerous Ancient Manuscripts in Hebrew, Latin, and French... New Age/Occult Pages 92

Rubaiyat Of Omar Khayyam *by Edward Fitzgerald* ISBN:*1-59462-332-5* **$13.95**
Edward Fitzgerald, whom the world has already learned, in spite of his own efforts to remain within the shadow of anonymity, to look upon as one of the rarest poets of the century, was born at Bredfield, in Suffolk, on the 31st of March, 1809. He was the third son of John Purcell... Music Pages 172

Ancient Law *by Henry Maine* ISBN: *1-59462-128-4* **$29.95**
The chief object of the following pages is to indicate some of the earliest ideas of mankind, as they are reflected in Ancient Law, and to point out the relation of those ideas to modern thought. Religiom/History Pages 452

Far-Away Stories *by William J. Locke* ISBN: *1-59462-129-2* **$19.45**
"Good wine needs no bush, but a collection of mixed vintages does. And this book is just such a collection. Some of the stories I do not want to remain buried for ever in the museum files of dead magazine-numbers an author's not unpardonable vanity..." Fiction Pages 272

Life of David Crockett *by David Crockett* ISBN: *1-59462-250-7* **$27.45**
"Colonel David Crockett was one of the most remarkable men of the times in which he lived. Born in humble life, but gifted with a strong will, an indomitable courage, and unremitting perseverance... Biographies/New Age Pages 424

Lip-Reading *by Edward Nitchie* ISBN: *1-59462-206-X* **$25.95**
Edward B. Nitchie, founder of the New York School for the Hard of Hearing, now the Nitchie School of Lip-Reading, Inc, wrote "LIP-READING Principles and Practice". The development and perfecting of this meritorious work on lip-reading was an undertaking... How-to Pages 400

A Handbook of Suggestive Therapeutics, Applied Hypnotism, Psychic Science ISBN: *1-59462-214-0* **$24.95**
by Henry Munro Health/New Age/Health/Self-help Pages 376

A Doll's House: and Two Other Plays *by Henrik Ibsen* ISBN: *1-59462-112-8* **$19.95**
Henrik Ibsen created this classic when in revolutionary 1848 Rome. Introducing some striking concepts in playwriting for the realist genre, this play has been studied the world over. Fiction/Classics/Plays 308

The Light of Asia *by sir Edwin Arnold* ISBN: *1-59462-204-3* **$13.95**
In this poetic masterpiece, Edwin Arnold describes the life and teachings of Buddha. The man who was to become known as Buddha to the world was born as Prince Gautama of India but he rejected the worldly riches and abandoned the reigns of power when... Religion/History/Biographies Pages 170

The Complete Works of Guy de Maupassant *by Guy de Maupassant* ISBN: *1-59462-157-8* **$16.95**
"For days and days, nights and nights, I had dreamed of that first kiss which was to consecrate our engagement, and I knew not on what spot I should put my lips..." Fiction/Classics Pages 240

The Art of Cross-Examination *by Francis L. Wellman* ISBN: *1-59462-309-0* **$26.95**
Written by a renowned trial lawyer, Wellman imparts his experience and uses case studies to explain how to use psychology to extract desired information through questioning. How-to/Science/Reference Pages 408

Answered or Unanswered? *by Louisa Vaughan* ISBN: *1-59462-248-5* **$10.95**
Miracles of Faith in China Religion Pages 112

The Edinburgh Lectures on Mental Science (1909) *by Thomas* ISBN: *1-59462-008-3* **$11.95**
This book contains the substance of a course of lectures recently given by the writer in the Queen Street Hall, Edinburgh. Its purpose is to indicate the Natural Principles governing the relation between Mental Action and Material Conditions... New Age/Psychology Pages 148

Ayesha *by H. Rider Haggard* ISBN: *1-59462-301-5* **$24.95**
Verily and indeed it is the unexpected that happens! Probably if there was one person upon the earth from whom the Editor of this, and of a certain previous history, did not expect to hear again... Classics Pages 380

Ayala's Angel *by Anthony Trollope* ISBN: *1-59462-352-X* **$29.95**
The two girls were both pretty, but Lucy who was twenty-one who supposed to be simple and comparatively unattractive, whereas Ayala was credited, as her Bombwhat romantic name might show, with poetic charm and a taste for romance. Ayala when her father died was nineteen... Fiction Pages 484

The American Commonwealth *by James Bryce* ISBN: *1-59462-286-8* **$34.45**
An interpretation of American democratic political theory. It examines political mechanics and society from the perspective of Scotsman James Bryce Politics Pages 572

Stories of the Pilgrims *by Margaret P. Pumphrey* ISBN: *1-59462-116-0* **$17.95**
This book explores pilgrims religious oppression in England as well as their escape to Holland and eventual crossing to America on the Mayflower, and their early days in New England... History Pages 268

www.bookjungle.com *email: sales@bookjungle.com fax: 630-214-0564 mail: Book Jungle PO Box 2226 Champaign, IL 61825*

QTY

The Fasting Cure *by Sinclair Upton* ISBN: *1-59462-222-1* **$13.95**

In the Cosmopolitan Magazine for May, 1910, and in the Contemporary Review (London) for April, 1910, I published an article dealing with my experiences in fasting. I have written a great many magazine articles, but never one which attracted so much attention... New Age/Self Help/Health Pages 164

Hebrew Astrology *by Sepharial* ISBN: *1-59462-308-2* **$13.45**

In these days of advanced thinking it is a matter of common observation that we have left many of the old landmarks behind and that we are now pressing forward to greater heights and to a wider horizon than that which represented the mind-content of our progenitors... Astrology Pages 144

Thought Vibration or The Law of Attraction in the Thought World ISBN: *1-59462-127-6* **$12.95**

by William Walker Atkinson Psychology/Religion Pages 144

Optimism *by Helen Keller* ISBN: *1-59462-108-X* **$15.95**

Helen Keller was blind, deaf, and mute since 19 months old, yet famously learned how to overcome these handicaps, communicate with the world, and spread her lectures promoting optimism. An inspiring read for everyone... Biographies/Inspirational Pages 84

Sara Crewe *by Frances Burnett* ISBN: *1-59462-360-0* **$9.45**

In the first place, Miss Minchin lived in London. Her home was a large, dull, tall one, in a large, dull square, where all the houses were alike, and all the sparrows were alike, and where all the door-knockers made the same heavy sound... Childrens/Classic Pages 88

The Autobiography of Benjamin Franklin *by Benjamin Franklin* ISBN: *1-59462-135-7* **$24.95**

The Autobiography of Benjamin Franklin has probably been more extensively read than any other American historical work, and no other book of its kind has had such ups and downs of fortune. Franklin lived for many years in England, where he was agent... Biographies/History Pages 332

Name	
Email	
Telephone	
Address	
City, State ZIP	

☐ Credit Card   ☐ Check / Money Order

Credit Card Number	
Expiration Date	
Signature	

Please Mail to: Book Jungle
PO Box 2226
Champaign, IL 61825
or Fax to: 630-214-0564

ORDERING INFORMATION

web*: www.bookjungle.com*
email*: sales@bookjungle.com*
fax*: 630-214-0564*
mail*: Book Jungle PO Box 2226 Champaign, IL 61825*
or PayPal *to sales@bookjungle.com*

Please contact us for bulk discounts

DIRECT-ORDER TERMS

20% Discount if You Order Two or More Books
Free Domestic Shipping!
Accepted: Master Card, Visa,
Discover, American Express

www.ingramcontent.com/pod-product-compliance
Lightning Source LLC
Chambersburg PA
CBHW080823020726
47501CB00009B/2401